A Colony of the World

A Colony of the World:
The United States Today

America's senior statesman warns his countrymen.

Eugene McCarthy

HIPPOCRENE BOOKS
NEW YORK

For information, address:
HIPPOCRENE BOOKS, INC.
171 Madison Avenue
New York, NY 10016

Library of Congress Cataloging-in-Publication Data
McCarthy, Eugene J., 1916 -
    A colony of the world : the United States today : America's senior
statesman warns his countrymen / Eugene McCarthy.
        p.   cm.
    Includes index.
    ISBN 0-7818-0102-8 (cloth)
    1. United States—Politics and government—1989- 2. United
States—Foreign relations—1989- 3. United States—Politics and
government—1981-1989. 4. United States—Foreign
relations—1981-1989. I. Title.
E881.M36   1992
973.928—dc20   92-26128
                CIP

Printed in the United States of America.

*Sincere appreciation to Rodney Huey,
who pulled this manuscript together.*

Contents

Introduction

CLASSICAL, HISTORICAL COLONIALISM IS MARKED BY DISTINCTIVE CHAR-
acteristics—political, military, economic, demographic and cultural.
Politically and militarily a colony is usually dependent in greater or
lesser degree upon the determinations and directions of its controlling country.

Economically and culturally colonial status is evident in loss of
control over borders, both as to the movement of goods and people,
and commonly over religion and language.

Major investment in a colony is from outside, with control held
by the investing powers. The colony is usually a supplier of raw
materials to the mother country and a purchaser of manufactured
goods, and its economy and financial institutions operate within
the monetary system of the mother country, controlling nations or
institutions.

It is the thesis of this book that the United States is now in a
colonial relationship, perhaps better labeled as in neo-colonial relations, not to one country or dominating nation, but to a combination
of outside forces (some political, some economic, some ideological)
and inside forces, which combine to bring us to colonial status.

PART I

CHAPTER I

Foreign Policy

THE MOST DISTURBING MARK OF THE COLONIALISM, OR NEO-COLONIAL-ism, of the United States is our loss of control over our foreign and military policy. The change from full and independent sovereignty and control of both foreign and military policy was not sudden, or dramatic, or historically noted. We did not become subject to another power as a result of conquest or surrender. Our movement into colonial status was subtle, gradual, largely unnoted, and principally of our own making. The movement into colonial dependency became noticeable in the early 1950s, when John Foster Dulles, as Secretary of State in the Eisenhower Administration, set his ideological mark upon United States foreign policy and its complementary military policy, and in effect took that policy out of the range of historical context, control and reality.

United States foreign policy until the Eisenhower years in the White House was relatively clear, direct and limited. The foreign policy of the United States from the end of World War II until the 1950s reflected and responded to international realities. The NATO treaty was agreed to and that organization created as a formal agreement among the nations of the Atlantic community to stand up against a real, rationally identified threat from Russia. The emphasis in forming the organization was on Russia, rather than on any abstract threat from communist ideology or monolithic world communism. The Marshall Plan, too, was designed to meet immediate, understandable and historically defined problems. The Truman Doctrine of Containment, as it was called, was not speculatively

3

conceived in an historical vacuum, but was a declaration of policy to help maintain the independence of Greece and Turkey.

The range and limits of foreign policy during the Truman Administration were set out in a speech given by Secretary of State Dean Acheson in these words: "We can never reach the point where all ends must be justified by their means before implementing policy, but we must be certain that our ends are really what we want. I take it as clear that where an important purpose of diplomacy is to further enduring good relations between states, the methods, the modes of conduct by which relations between nations are carried on must be designed to inspire trust and confidence. To achieve this result, the conduct of diplomacy should conform to the same moral and ethical principles which inspire trust and confidence when followed by and between individuals."

Truman's concept of national defense was one of a defined line, described most simply when he said, "anytime a pig sticks its snout under, the thing to do is hit it on the snout."

The approach to foreign policy that developed during the Eisenhower years, under the Dulles influence, was quite different from that which had been followed in the Truman Administration. It was aggressive, arrogant, dominating, moralistic and ideological.

To Dulles, neutralism was not a defensible position for any country. It was simply "immoral." Communism was not, for Dulles, a historical reality, but it was, he held, in the minds of its advocates and believers "the wave of the future." He held we must counter by "having a people on our side who believe that our way of life is the wave of the future."

To Dulles, communism was a monolith and international communism a single party. He conceived foreign policy in broad moral terms such as peace and liberation and made threats not of retaliation, but of "massive retaliation."

"Our foreign policy can best be expressed," he wrote, "by extending to the whole world the words of the Preamble to the Constitution of the United States, to form a more perfect union, establish justice, insure domestic tranquility, provide for the common defense, promote the general welfare, and secure the blessings of liberty to ourselves and our posterity. . . ."

What does this mean in our international relations?

"To form a more perfect union" means to assist in making the United Nations an effective organization for peace. "Establish justice" means to strengthen international law to bring peace with justice. "Insure domestic tranquility" means to assist other peoples to achieve their just aspirations through peaceful change rather than violence. "Provide for the common defense" means to join with other nations to protect their freedom and ours from any force, particularly international communism, which seeks to destroy them. "Promote the general welfare" means to stimulate the development of the less developed nations. "Secure the blessings of liberty" embraces all of these objectives, and it also means we should make known to other peoples that the American Revolution was the true revolution for human freedom.

The idealism of Dulles, bordering on fanaticism, should not have surprised anyone who knew his background, which was basically religious, moralistic and legalistic. Strains of Calvinism ran strongly in his conscience and in his views of politics and of government. For generations his family on his father's side had been involved in religious activities. Among his ancestors were a number of ministers, including missionaries to India and Ceylon.

His father was a Presbyterian minister and his mother was from a legal political family. Dulles was a friend of Henry Luce, who had been born in China to Christian missionaries. Congressman Walter Judd, who had been a Presbyterian medical missionary to China, was his confidant and adviser on Chinese communist matters, including the question of Alger Hiss' loyalty. By report, Dulles' family expected him to become a minister, but he chose law believing he could do more good as a "Christian lawyer." This choice was comparable to that of John Calvin, who after becoming a priest, became a lawyer.

In dealing with foreign policy, Dulles combined zeal and covenanting, combining what he saw as moral and legal obligations. Although Dulles, earlier in his career, had expressed skepticism about the value of international treaties and accords, he proceeded almost immediately following his taking office as Secretary of State to take up treaty making. He became a great covenanter. During his service as Secretary of State, SEATO, the South Eastern Asia Treaty Organization was established. Mutual defense treaties with Korea, with Nationalist China and with Japan were agreed to. The United States, although not a formal member of the Bagdad Pact, committed itself to support of the purposes of the Pact. There was talk of a mid-East African treaty or agreement, including Israel, Somalia and Ethiopia, sustained by the United States, as a means of containing Egypt's Nasser. Only Central and South were spared additional treaty control. Evidently, Dulles considered The Organization of American States, with a fallback to the Monroe Doctrine, as adequate.

In addition to promoting treaties and advocating the endorsement of the Bagdad Pact, Dulles was a strong and persistent promoter of congressional resolutions, either in support of current policies or in anticipation of future policies or actions.

These resolutions served Dulles' purposes in two ways: first, by giving a legalistic (covenanted) basis for actions, and second, by blunting or preventing congressional criticism.

President Truman sent United States forces into Korea to help repel an attack on South Korea by North Koreans without any covering congressional approval. According to Dean Acheson, a protective resolution was proposed to President Truman who rejected it with an assertion that what he was doing was clearly within the range of his rights and responsibilities and that he would stand against the critics, as in fact he did.

Dulles, on the contrary, was quick to come to Congress for resolutions in support of foreign policy initiative. Thus, in 1955 he secured the adoption of the Far East (Formosa) resolution. The function and purpose of the resolution was explained by Dulles as follows: "With Formosa threatened with attack from the Chinese mainland, we got the Far East resolution passed by Congress. This put the Peking government unmistakably on notice that if it attacked Formosa, the United States would instantly be in the war."

The resolution, he said, covered not only Formosa, but also the Pescadores and related positions and territories of that area that were in friendly hands.

More significant than the Far East Resolution was the Middle East Resolution, approved by Congress in 1957, which authorized the president to cooperate with and assist any nation or group of nations of the Middle East desiring assistance in developing economic and military strength dedicated to the maintenance of national independence and protecting themselves against armed aggression from a communist dominated country.

Whereas there was little opposition to the Far East Resolution, which was directed at a defined and limited target, significant opposition to the Middle East Resolution arose in the Congress.

Opponents of the resolution properly charged that it was something of a blank check, to be used in unidentified circumstances. The vote in the Senate was 72 for and 19 against. The vote in the House of Representatives was 355 for and 61 against.

The effect of resolutions of this kind was not only to give the president advance approval for undefined actions, but to give to the House of Representatives standing on foreign policy matters substantially equal to the constitutionally-designed special power of the Senate.

The third major resolution bearing on foreign policy was the Gulf of Tonkin Resolution adopted in August 1964, during the interim Johnson Administration, following the death of President Kennedy and the election of November 1964. It was similar in its effect and purpose to the Far East and Middle East Resolution of the Eisenhower presidency. The secretary of state who promoted it was Dean Rusk. Rusk's approach to foreign policy and his basic ideas were similar to those of John Foster Dulles. Rusk, like the father of Dulles, had been a Presbyterian minister. Rusk had special interest in the Far East, having served in the China-India-Burma theater under General Stillwell in 1943. He had been deputy under secretary of state in 1949 and 1950 and assisting secretary for Far Eastern Affairs from 1950 to 1952. In this office he had in 1951 hailed U.S. policy in support of Chiang Kai-shek, declaring that the Peking government "is not the government of China," and that the Nationalist government "more authentically represents the views of the great body of people of China."

A third device, further limiting freedom and independence of judgment in historical context was the rise of the presidential doctrine, usually nonofficial and non-formal, but declared to be by president or members of an administration, and confirmed by the press or declared to exist by the press itself.

The power of the doctrine had its origin in the Monroe Doctrine. That doctrine grew out of a statement made to the Congress by President Monroe on December 22, 1823. President Monroe did not know that he was proclaiming a "doctrine," or if he did, he did not say that he was. From the record, it seems that he thought he was making a statement of policy relative to what he thought was possible foreign intervention in Central and South America. Monroe's statement, which later became a doctrine, was a simple warning, stated in these words:

"With the existing colonies or dependencies of any European power, we have not interfered, and shall not interfere. But with the governments who have declared their independence, and maintained it, and whose independence we have on great consideration and on just principles acknowledged, we could not view any interposition for the purpose of oppressing them, controlling in any other manner, their destiny, by any European power, in any other light, than as the manifestation of an unfriendly disposition toward the United States."

President Kennedy has been credited with having formulated two doctrines, although he did not label them as doctrines at the time of formulation.

The first, a highly personal and broad one contained in his inaugural address, asserted that the United States would "pay any price, bear any burden, meet any hardship, support any friend, oppose any foe, in order to assure the survival and the success of liberty."

This doctrine was directed at preserving an old order. President Bush has proclaimed a similar doctrine in the interest of a new world order.

The second Kennedy doctrine, undeclared and unstated, was induced to justify the invasion of Cuba. This doctrine incorporated elements of the Monroe Doctrine, although the invading force was not a foreign army but a foreign ideology, and elements of the Eisenhower Middle Eastern doctrine transferred to the Western Hemisphere principally the right, if not the obligation, to interfere if called upon by a recognized non-communist government, no matter how tenuous that government might be or how limited its controlled territory might be. A beachhead, in the case of Cuba, was judged adequate.

Two additional forces, approaching doctrinal status, have been brought to bear on foreign policy determination, both tending to isolate policy from challenge or critical examination.

The first, which may fairly be called the Johnson doctrine, quickly endorsed and adopted by Richard Nixon after he became president, held that an incumbent had the right, if not the duty, to carry on policies initiated or advanced by a preceding president or presidents. President Johnson offered, as support for his continuing and escalating the war in Vietnam, the fact that the war had in some direct or indirect way been supported by the three presidents preceding him in office: Truman had aided the French when they were fighting the Viet Cong; Eisenhower had sent in military advisers numbering about 900 persons; and President Kennedy had sent 17,000 or more special forces personnel. Subsequently, President Nixon stated that

he was only carrying on what four presidents before him had supported.

What may become known as the Nixon doctrine was implicit in
that administration's military move into Cambodia without form or
informal treaty, resolution or doctrine. The move was called an
incursion. It was the first identified incursion conducted by the
United States in our history. An incursion differs from an invasion.
There is no verb form of the word. One cannot "incurse" as one
can invade. An incursion is a kind of existential happening, without
a before or after; it is a continuum. An extension of the doctrine
might allow each president one incursion, as for example, President
Reagan's incursion into Grenada and President Bush's into Panama.

CHAPTER II

Military

THE SECOND MAJOR FORCE THAT HAS CONDITIONED UNITED STATES FOR-
eign policy, insulating it from clear rational judgment in historical
context over the last three decades and complementing the anti-
communist oversimplified ideology of Dulles and others, has been
the military one.

This force has been and is made up of two major factors: one, that
of the actual military establishment, labeled the "military-industrial
complex" by President Eisenhower in his farewell address on leaving
the presidency; and two, the covering and sustaining theories of
military strategy and geopolitics.

Alexis de Tocqueville in his book *Democracy in America* warned of
the danger to a democracy of a military establishment that was
larger, stronger or more powerful than was needed for immediate
or reasonable predictable military action. Such a force, he warned,
would become a political force in itself and exercise great influence
on the democratic society which it was designed to serve, if it in
fact did not come to control that society. At the time de Tocqueville
made his observations, the United States military was a limited
power, having only minimal influence on domestic or foreign policy.

In 1831, the year de Tocqueville visited the United States, the
number of active duty enlisted personnel was 9,913, of which 5,442
were in the army and 3,691 in the navy. The numbers increased to
approximately 50,000 at the time of the Mexican War with about
40,000 in the army and 10,000 in the navy and 1,700 Marines. There
was no accurate count of forces in the army during the Civil War,
but the number in the navy and the marines totaled about 55,000

persons. From the end of the Civil War until the Spanish-American War, the total number in the armed forces varied from approximately 35,000 to 40,000. During World War I, peak enrollment occurred in 1918 when the number of persons in the army was recorded over 2,265,000 and in the combined navy and marines over 465,000. The numbers quickly declined after the war and hovered in the 300,000 range from 1920 until 1940.

In 1945 enlisted personnel on active duty for World War II totaled 10,795,775. By 1947 the number was down to 1,385,436 and remained at about that level until the Korean War when the number increased to a high of 3,254,790 in 1952; the army having 1,446,266 persons, the navy 738,451, the marines 215,554, and the air force 854,519. The number increased to over 3,000,000 during the Vietnam War. Following that war the number of persons in the military leveled off at about 2,000,000.

Within the complex of persons with ties to the military establishment are some 1,155,000 civilian employees; 1,660,810 reservists as of 1989; dependent persons numbering over 1,000,000 in that same year; plus over 1,300,000 retired military annuitants.

It was not until after the end of World War II and the Korean War that anything comparable to the kind of establishment that de Tocqueville warned against developed in the United States. It did not spring full blown from the war itself. In the interim between the end of World War II and the beginning of the Korean War, defense budgets were reduced to as low as $15–$16 billion a year. Defense expenditures to meet the costs of the Korean War rose to $40 billion and more annually, and did not come down after the war, rising to approximately $100 billion a year by 1978; to $200 billion by 1988; and to over $300 billion by 1990, in advance of increases resulting from the war in the Persian Gulf area.

Before World War II, ships were built in the U.S. Navy yard. Tanks were built in factories operated by the army. There were naval gun and torpedo factories, army arsenals and munitions plants, and no air force.

Major involvement of civilian productive industries came with World War II, which was a war of supply, production and logistics, requiring much more material and service than could be provided by the military operating on its own. The whole United States industrial, transportation and service establishment was mobilized in support of the war. Privately owned shipyards built ships for the navy. Automobile companies became manufacturers of tanks and of jeeps. Private companies expanded production of guns and of ammunition. The air services, which had no separate existence until after the war, was almost wholly dependent on nonmilitary suppliers.

De Tocqueville, with all of his marvelous gift of foresight, could scarcely have been expected to anticipate how accurately the Pentagon, covering label for the whole military-industrial complex with its outside support, fulfilled his forecast, becoming a kind of republic within the republic, with its own welfare program (including health care and an educational system; housing, recreational and retirement programs; veterinary services, even though the cavalry is gone, and only the canine corps, some experimental animals, dolphins and homing pigeons remain in the service; and the PX, which became the largest retail operation in the country, or of the country, behind Sears-Roebuck).

The full extent of this duplication or replication of civilian life and culture by the military became evident in the debate on the first Reagan defense budget, in which it was found that the administration while cutting other elements in the budget, both military and nonmilitary, not only planned no cuts in money for military bands and other musical units, but that on the contrary, it was proposing an increase in the appropriation. The involvement of the military culture with general culture was demonstrated in the congressional debate about the appropriation as the proposed increase came under attack from three definable interests.

The first group was the pure budget cutters, a subspecies which holds that if the budget is cut anywhere it should be cut everywhere, without distinction or prejudice. They held that if the fat was to be omitted from the defense budget, then military music should be muted, too. If the nation could get along with fewer food stamps and not so many MX missiles, they asked, why can't it get along with fewer tubas?

The second line of attack was from members of Congress who had risen above financial considerations where the defense budget was concerned, but questioned the impact of music upon national security. Some of these—the militarists who fear that the West is losing the will to resist—had heard that "music hath charms to soothe the savage beast." They worried that too much, especially of the gentler or the more syncopated music played by some military ensembles, might dull the military spirit.

The third front on which the military musicians were besieged was manned and womanned by lovers of better music and the higher culture. They did not argue directly against the military bands appropriations, but made the relative argument that these outlays should not be increased, if, as recommended by the Reagan Administration, the appropriation for support of the civilian arts was to be cut by 50 percent to a mere $77 million, approximately $13 million less than that being proposed for the uniformed instrumentalists. Senator Edward Kennedy, in a letter asking for contributions to his Fund for a Democratic Majority, made a special point of calling attention to these budget items. He wrote, "The new military budget, for example, contains more money—$89.9 million—for military bands than the entire budget proposed for the National Endowment for the Arts." And, Representative Fred Richmond of New York, addressing the same point, said, "There are three full (military) bands in the Washington area, and each of them has a larger budget than the National Symphony Orchestra," and added, "I don't think it's fair."

Whether the appropriations were unfair is open to challenge. Obviously they were not equitable in comparison with those proposed for the National Endowment for the Arts. But the case against the military music appropriations could successfully be made on grounds of equity and fairness. There were deeper and more complex forces operating here.

Maintaining separate musical units has always been a mark of pride and of practicality among the separate services. The popularity of the Marine Band was a formidable obstacle when the Pentagon, during the early 1960s, attempted to liquidate the Marine Corps. Secretary of Defense Robert McNamara, in his efforts to unify the armed forces, never got to the point of trying to unify the bands. He was routed far earlier. But it was suspected that he did have long-range contingency plans for an eventual try at melding the musical groups of the branches of the armed forces. These plans were never activated, possibly because of the failure of his effort to provide one fighter airplane, originally known as the TFX, which, it was projected, would satisfy the needs of all branches of the armed services.

It was not only separation among the forces that was at issue, but also the competition among them. The growth of music appropriations for the armed forces reflected general growth in military spending and the rivalry among the services for possession and control of weapons and weapons systems.

In arms competition, each branch of our armed forces seeks to be fully prepared to carry out the three kinds of possible military action, defined by the Pentagon as conventional war, unconventional (nuclear) war and irregular guerrilla war. In the realm of music they seek to be similarly flexible.

The bedrock of musical preparedness is, of course, the conventional military band. In this category are the basic marching bands of the U.S. Army, the Navy, the Air Force and the Marine Corps. Like the Pentagon itself, these bands tend to be heavy on the brass. The army has 50 basic bands. The navy has 17, some of which are equipped with life jackets. The marine corps has 10. And the air Force has 20, which can be divided into roughly three kinds, comparable to bombing wings, fighter wings and missile emplacements.

In addition to the marching bands, the separate services each have a variety of unconventional and irregular musical groups. On the choral front, the army is clearly ahead since it can call upon the massed vocal power of the U.S. Army Chorus. The navy has the Sea Chanters and the Air Force has the Singing Sergeants. In the jazz theater of operations, the army deploys a unit known as the Army Blues, the navy's able-bodied jazzmen are called The Commodores and the Air Force, at a moment's notice, can scramble a jazz combo called Airmen of Note.

The army, in its diversified musical arsenal, has a chamber orchestra, a brass quartet, a string quarter, a unit called the Herald Trumpets (specializing in fanfares) and a fife and drum corps.

The navy counters with an elite instrumental combo, Cross Current. The navy also has a country bluegrass group and Port Authority which plays rock 'n roll. The latter groups, the navy says, are used principally for recruiting. The navy has no string group, leaving a dangerous window of vulnerability in its Montovani-class strike force. The air force, however, partially closes the gap with The Strolling Strings. The air force also has a rapid deployment rock band called Mach I. It once had a unit of Scottish pipes, now discontinued in favor of all-weather musical technology.

The marine corps makes a point of not breaking its musicians into specialized units. This is consistent with the corps' tradition of going anywhere and of doing anything it is called upon to do. Its spokesperson says that members of the marine band can be selected on request to perform any kind of musical mission from Bach to rock, from band to orchestra, combo and ensemble to solo work on instruments like guitar and harp, from the halls of Montezuma to (as seems increasingly likely) the shores of Tripoli and on to the Persian Gulf.

The military-industrial establishment, as a powerful influence on domestic and foreign policy, did not come into being as an afterthought or incidental development from the war.

Long before the complex was in place, in fact scarcely before World War II had ended, there was evidence that the military and those interested in it had plans for the future. An executive committee, the Woodrum Committee, made recommendations to Congress which took up the recommendations and passed reorganization legislation in 1947 and again in 1949. The report accompanying the 1947 legislation stated that out of hearings and studies of the preceding years had come general agreement that the military organization should be built around a "tightly knit core of land, sea and air power." "The difficulty" the report went on to say, "lay not in determining whether, but how closely, these three major branches of our military strength should be interfaced." With the passage of the 1949 legislation, two highly significant changes were approved bearing on future military power, influence and operations.

The first was the firm, legal establishment of the U.S. Air Force as a military department within the Department of Defense, with status equal to that of the Departments of the Army and of the Navy. Air power advocates, riding on the popularity achieved by air power as an element of the army and the navy during World War II, prevailed despite opposition from the Army Department, and especially the Navy Department. Establishing the third department resolved the dispute between the army and the navy relative to unification. Each department evidently believed that with the unification one or the other would dominate the new unified department. The new plan introduced the principle of the trinity, with the internal assurance that any two of the three departments could unite against the third if it threatened to become dominant.

The second provision of the 1947 and 1949 legislation bearing on the continuing force of the military was the abandonment of the word "war" in the general department title, and replacing it with the less aggressive, but more enduring and unassailable word "defense." The need for a large war department might be challenged if there were no war, or a demand on a war department to report its war plans. A defense department could not fairly be subjected to such challenges or demands. Moreover, the demands for defense are potentially without limit. No matter how thorough its defense efforts were the animal in Kafka's story "The Burrow" remained fearful and insecure. A scratching sound was disturbing, as was silence.

The military-industrial complex was further strengthened through procurement policies that added a powerful political factor through the widespread distribution of defense contracts and subcontracts. The procurement program for building the air force's B-2 is an example. As originally conceived, the procurement would have been distributed among 46 states, with the possibility that 92 senators would have had some interest in the economic fallout of the program which had the potential of supplying work to tens of thousands of workers, and contracts to hundreds of suppliers. The prime contractors were Northrop Corporation; key subcontractors were Boeing, LTV, General Electric and Hughes Companies who were to receive additional subcontracts or sub-subcontracts, according to the Defense Department, on a state-by-state basis were as follows:

Arizona
    Allied Signal Aerospace
    Allied Signal Fluid Systems Division
    Garrett Auxiliary Power, Inc.

California
    Allied Signal Aerospace, Air Research, L.A.
    Allied Consulting & Tech Service
    Associate N/C Programming
    B & H Associates
    Burns & Roe Pacific Engineers
    Condor Systems, Inc.
    Deliotte, Haskins & Sells
    Evolving Technology
    Ewing Technical Design, Inc.
    Explosive Technology, Inc.
    Facilities Systems Engineering
    Frequency West
    GEC Astronics Corporation
    General Dynamics Electronic Division
    Gould Defense Systems
    Hughes Aircraft, Radar System Group
    Hughes Electronic Dynamics
    Hughes Training & Control Division
    Inconen Corporation

ITT Gilfillan
Jaycor
Kaymar
Lockheed Aircraft Corporation
Mantech Support Technologies, Inc.
McDonnell Douglas Aircraft, Inc.
Mini Systems
Mini Systems Associates
Multax Systems
Narda Microwave, Inc.
Norman Engineering Co.
Parker Hannifin
PDA Engineering
Raychem Corporation
Raytheon Co.
Resdel Engineering Corporation
Servicon Systems, Inc.
Spectragraphic Corporation
Sundstrand
TAD Tech Services Corporation
Teledyne Electronics
Teledyne McCormick
Texas Instruments Ridgecrest
TRW, Redondo Beach
TRW, Sacramento Engineering Office
TRW Space & Defense
UTS Engineering & Consultants
VERAC, Inc.
Watkins-Johnson Co.
Whittaker Corporation

Colorado
General Devices, Inc.
Kaman Instrumention
Kaman Sciences Corporation
Mantecs
OEA, Inc.
Storage Tech Corporation
Stonehouse Group
Unisys Corporation Defense Systems

Connecticut
  Amaco Performance Products
  Ensign Bickford Co.
  Hamilton Standard
  Tech Systems Corporation

District of Columbia
  McKenna, Conner & Cuneo

Florida
  Hi Tec
  United Technologies

Georgia
  Electromagnetic Devices

Idaho
  Vanite Industries

Illinois
  Electrodynamics, Inc.
  Sundstrand Aviation

Iowa
  Rockwell International Corporation, Collins Division

Kansas
  Boeing Military Airplane Co.

Kentucky
  Keco Industries, Inc.

Maryland
  AAI Corporation
  Digital Equipment
  Fairchild Communications & Electronics Co.

Massachusetts
  Adage, Inc.
  Adams-Russell Co., Inc.
  Adams-Russell Electronics Co., Inc.

Fenwal, Inc.
General Electric Aircraft Equipment Division
Kaman Avidyne
Lighting Technologies
Microdynamics, Inc.
Microwave Associates, Inc.
Microwave Development Labs
Microwave Engineering Corporation
Varian

Michigan
Smith Industries Aerospace & Defense

Minnesota
Honeywell
Rosemount, Inc.
Unisys Corporation, Defense Systems

New Hampshire
Continental Microwave & Tool Co.
Kom Wave Corporation
Sanders Associates, Inc.
Tech Resources, Inc.

New Jersey
Allied Corporation, Bendix Flight System
Kearfott Guidance/Navigation Corporation
Lockheed Electronics, Inc.
Micro Lab

New Mexico
Los Alamos Technical Associates, Inc.

New York
Arkwin Industries, Inc.
Eastman Kodak
General Electric Aircraft Controls
Gull, Inc.
Hazeltine
Miltope Co.
Moog, Inc.

Scipar, Inc.
Transportable Technology, Inc.

Ohio
  Battelle Columbus
  BDM Corporation
  General Electric Aircraft Engineering Group
  Logicon

Oklahoma
  Defense Technologies, Inc.
  TRW Oklahoma Engineering Office

Texas
  B&M Associates
  Belcan Services
  Butler Service Group
  Consultants & Designers, Inc.
  Contract Services
  E-Systems
  Ernst & Whitney
  General Devices
  H.L. Yoh
  International Business Machines
  Interglobal Technical Services
  LTV Aircraft Products Group
  LTV Missiles & Electronics Group
  N/C Services
  Nelson, Coulson & Associates, Inc.
  PDS-Tech Services
  Pollack & San
  Rockwell International Corporation
  Standard Manufacturing Co.
  Superior Manufacturing Co.
  Superior Design Co., Inc.
  TAD Technical Services
  Versatec
  Wang

Utah
  Hercules, Inc.

Vermont
  Hercules Aerospace
  Simmonds Precision

Virginia
  Amdahl Federal Service Corporation
  Mantech International Corporation
  Xerox

Washington
  Boeing Military Advanced Systems Co.
  Eldec Corporation
  Ewing Tech Design, Inc.
  General Electric
  Kirk-Mayer, Inc.
  Nelson, Coulson & Associates, Inc.
  RHO Co., Inc.
  Science & Engineering Associates, Inc.
  VTC Service Corporation

The fourth prop or support of the military industrial complex was put in place when the draft law was allowed to expire in the Nixon Administration, to be replaced with what was called The Volunteer Army program. In the post-Vietnam period, both militarists and civil libertarians looked for an alternative to the flawed and discriminatory draft program that was in effect during the closing years of the Vietnam War. The militarists argued that under the volunteer (better called mercenary) program only those who wanted to be in the military, or were willing to enter it for money, would enter the military services. The anti-militarists and the libertarians were satisfied that under the new program those who wished to stay out of the military would be free to do so. Both sides seemed either unfamiliar with the admonition of de Tocqueville, relative to the dangers of a mercenary army, or unfamiliar, or indifferent, to the debate between Hamilton and Jefferson, when the nation was being established. Hamilton wanted a mercenary, professional army and Jefferson held for a citizen's army drawn from the public. Neither Hamilton or Jefferson or their views prevailed until the 1970s. Until then our military forces had been a mixture of citizen and professional personnel, made up of a corps of professionals supplemented by a citizen's draft for major wars.

Although the war in the Persian Gulf area was not a clear test of the military, political and social implications or consequences of using a mercenary army, there is evidence that de Tocqueville's warning was worthy of attention, as it was argued by some that the military involved in the Gulf had questionable grounds for objecting to the war, since they had been paid, or were being paid, and that noncombatants and the public in general need not have much consideration for combatants who had contracted for military service.

Undergirding and sustaining the overall ideological justification for military confrontation with communism were more specific concepts and measurements as to what we needed in the way of military power to defeat or contain the Russians and their allies and dependencies. In the course of the last 30 years we have accepted and then discarded three such major concepts of security and superiority. In the campaign of 1960 it was charged that there was a missile gap, that we were behind the Russians in missile technology and production. The gap never quite reached the status of a controlling concept, especially when after the election the Democrats in power found that there was indeed a gap that favored the United States. Maintaining, possibly widening, the gap was then established as a rule for increasing defense procurement, especially of missiles and of nuclear weapons until a more compelling and more formal concept of measurement was introduced at some point during the term of Secretary of Defense Robert McNamara.

That standard was covered under the title of Mutual Assured Deterrence. In its early formulation it was based on the acceptance that if we could assure the Russians that we could destroy 20 percent of their important population centers and/or 50 percent of their industrial capacity the possibility alone would deter them from attacking us. Presumably, assurance that they could do the same to us would act as a comparable deterrent against the initiation of nuclear war on our part. No reasoned or historical evidence was introduced to sustain the 20 and 50 percent figures. They were a kind of secular revelation and dominated nuclear arms thinking, at least in the United States, until our arms buildup and that of the Russians reached a point at which each side not only had the potential to destroy the other's people and industrial capacity beyond the Mutual Assured Deterrence levels to 100 percent and even multiples of 100 percent.

A new measure was introduced. In the years immediately follow-ing the end of World War II and on into the 1960s, the words "strat-egy" and "strategic" carried traditional meaning, both as applied to military planning and actions. But by 1967 a change in application took place. In that year, the Johnson Administration approached the Soviet Union with a proposal to hold talks on Strategic Arms Limitations rather than, as one might have expected if the accepted meaning of strategy had been applied, on the arms limitations. In the new approach a distinction between "strategic" and "nonstrategic" weapons was introduced. The implication seemed to be that non-nuclear weapons now were purely tactical or just plain weapons. Distinctions were made first between conventional weapons and nu-clear weapons and then more subtly between conventional nuclear weapons and new, or non-conventional nuclear weapons. In this transition the weapon had come to define its function.

By the early 1970s, nuclear weapon thinkers began to talk about "strategic superiority" as a new measure of advance. Even those who introduced, or used the phrase, had difficulty explaining what it meant. When asked in 1974 what the term meant, Henry Kissinger reportedly said, "What in God's name is strategic superiority? What can you do with it?"

Five years later Kissinger said that he had spoken in a moment of pique in 1974 and that he did indeed know what constituted strategic superiority. Harold Brown, secretary of defense under President Nixon, took up the challenge of definition, declaring that "meaning superiority" (not ordinary superiority, mind you) was a "disparity in strategic capability" which, he said, can be "translated into political effect." He did not give figures. But gradually strategic superiority came to be measured in quantitative terms of how many more times can we kill all the Russians (all that count) than they could kill all the Americans that count.

The SALT II projection was that parity would be reached, under the terms of that agreement, when each side would have the potential to kill the other approximately 30 times over. This was a slight backdown from a projection of our military superiority by Melvin Laird, secretary of defense under Nixon, who had stated that our goal in defense buildup was to match and exceed what we knew the enemy had; then to match and exceed their estimated potential; and go beyond that to match and exceed what the momentum of their potential might produce.

As the 1980 campaign approached and the SALT II effort had failed, the multiples of reciprocal death lost appeal. A new guide or measure of security was introduced, namely the percentage of gross national product that we were spending on defense relative to the percentage of gross national product that the Russians were spending on defense. Five percent was the figure settled on as the break point.

According to the experts, if we spent less than five percent on our GNP on defense, we would fall behind and find ourselves in a "window of peril" by 1985. Some military experts were more refined in their calculations, insisting on percentages such as 5.23 percent and 5.25 percent. The case for the five percent break point was somewhat weakened when an expert on money and exchange rates asserted that if both the Russian and the United States GNP and defense expenditures were figured in rubles, the United States was quite secure, whereas if both GNPs and defense expenditures were figured in dollars, we were by the five percent standard slightly insecure. Thus arose the defining ironic situation whereby each country would be more secure if it judged its security in the currency of the other country, a comparison made more difficult since the ruble at that time was not being freely traded or convertible in the money markets of the world.

The percent of GNP spent on defense lingered on as an issue into the presidential debates of the 1984 campaign, although the percentage rose a few points above the five percent figure, and the imperative need for a 600-ship navy was added as an additional measure of security.

Loose ends and gaps in strategic thinking were tied up and filled out by principles of diplomatic relations and historical examples and references from contemporary or past experience and thought principally from the days of the Austro-Hungarian Empire, related to Europe—and the threat of a Communist China (yellow menace with a red tinge).

European policy was significantly influenced by the ideas of presidential advisers with Austro-Hungarian identification, ethnically, geographically and ideologically. China policy was influenced by what was called the "China Lobby"—a mixed body of China experts, missionaries and children of missionaries and declared anticommunists.

In the history of Western civilization, there have been periods during which political advisers, especially foreign policy advisers, were chosen because of their national background. Thus in the 16th century, possibly because of the writings of Machiavelli, it was widely believed by European rulers that they should have Italians to advise them in statecraft. British and Austrian consultants became popular in later centuries. The French had a short period of popularity after World War I.

The United States never adopted the European practice of attaching the foreigners directly to its government, but its policy was affected by the reputations of other nations for wisdom and expertness in foreign policy. After World War II, however, acting in the confidence of its power and successes and sense of rightness, if not righteousness, the United States developed a purely American foreign policy, directed by tested Americans and controlled by tried American principles. In the administrations of Presidents Truman, Eisenhower, Kennedy and Johnson, their secretaries of state were, of course, American born. They were drawn from the White Anglo-Saxon Protestant tradition of the United States. Moreover, Dean Acheson, John Foster Dulles and Dean Rusk also were the sons of Protestant divines with strong missionary spirit.

Beginning in the Johnson Administration and continuing into the administrations of Presidents Nixon and Carter, there was a change in preference. Nixon and Carter chose foreign policy advisers from areas in or adjacent to the territory formerly known as the Austro-Hungarian Empire. Johnson chose Walt Rostow.

Nixon chose Henry Kissinger, who was born in Germany, but within 20 or 30 miles of what were once the borders of the Austro-Hungarian Empire. Henry seems more Austrian than German, although he denied considering himself a modern Metternich. On the contrary, he said he had been much more deeply influenced by Kant and Spinoza (a combination of categorical imperative and Spinozan pantheism, one would have to conclude). Nevertheless, the similarities between Kissinger and Metternich are more obvious than similarities between him and Kant and Spinoza. Metternich was German born, as is Henry. Metternich was more Austrian than German in character, attitudes and manners. The same, I believe, can be said of Kissinger.

President Carter's foreign policy adviser, Zbigniew Brzezinski, was Polish-born. During the campaign of 1976, according to candidate Carter's issues coordinator Milton Gwirtzman, "We had to clear everything with Brzezinski that concerned foreign policy. Carter would ask: 'Has Brzezinski seen this?' So finally all staff memos on foreign policy had notes attached indicating that he had approved or seen them."

What were Brzezinski's views of himself, what was his overall view of world policy, what were his positions on foreign policy issues?

Brzezinski did not help us, as Kissinger did, by identifying himself with diplomats of the past, or with philosophers. He had not written a book quite comparable to Walt Rostow's *The Stages of Economic Growth,* indicating his general policies, giving us a basis for judging his policy against the thesis of a book and giving himself an opportunity to prove his thesis correct.

Brzezinski said that the Vietnam War was the "Waterloo of the elite" and suggested that, had the elite been firmly in control, the United States would have won the war. This elite, according to Brzezinski, was made up of the "WASP, Ivy-league-trained, Wall Street-based establishment operating through such institutions as the Council on Foreign Relations, but more pervasively." Brzezinski said that he was "very much part of the WASP community" and at the same time part of the intellectual community.

Thus we start with a secure person, by his own judgment, one who said that his policy would be architectural, not acrobatic, an obviously disapproving reference to the Kissinger methods or approach to foreign policy.

Perhaps more serious than the architectural approach was the rejection by Brzezinski and President Carter of the Kissinger "Lone Ranger" approach to foreign policy. This criticism of Kissinger I found hard to understand. The Lone Ranger was, insofar as I can recall, always successful. He accomplished his missions with a minimum of violence. He believed in justice and human rights. He got along well with Indians, especially with Tonto. And, it seems to me, things always worked out better when the Lone Ranger turned up than they would have worked out had the cavalry been sent.

Somewhat more disturbing, and more noteworthy, than Brzezinski's broad historical judgments and projections were his more particular judgments of record.

In speaking of the Columbia University student uprising of 1968, Brzezinski reportedly said that the authorities had not used sufficient force in putting down the uprising (certainly nothing like that used at Kent State two years later). Then he pronounced a great principle: that "the use of force must be designed not only to eliminate the surface revolutionary challenge but to make certain that the revolutionary forces cannot later rally again under the same leadership." (One can envision the burning of villages and the execution of a few relatives of the leaders.) He continued, "If that leadership cannot be physically liquidated, it can at least be expelled from the country or area in which the revolution is taking place." He later said that he was not advocating physical liquidation, but simply describing a logical alternative. (He described an alternative, but it is hard for me to understand why he said it was a logical one.) According to Scheer's account, Brzezinski went on to make clear that this analysis did not apply to the Columbia uprising itself.

Before the Czech uprising in 1968, Brzezinski said that the Czechs were too placid to revolt. He added, according to the Scheer article, that the United States should not encourage them to revolt—not because the revolt would be futile, which it was, but because it might be difficult for the United States to deal with an independent Czechoslovakia. Zbig, presumably an expert on the history of the Austro-Hungarian Empire and the Thirty Years' War, should not have so downgraded the Czechs. He should have remembered that day in 1618 when the Bohemian (Czech) noblemen, refusing to accept the elevation of Ferdinand of Styria as their ruler, broke into the room in which the imperial envoys were staying and hurled them out of the window into the castle moat some 60 feet below— an act known in history as the "defenestration of Prague." And he should have remembered that the Czechs took this action when Austrians and Hungarians appeared ready to accept, passively, the new ruler. So began the Thirty Years' War.

In February of 1968, Brzezinski, not an expert on Asia, had these words about Vietnam for *US News & World Report:* "Whether we like it or not, we are involved in something very long-term. . . . We must make it clear to the enemy that we have the staying power. . . . we're willing to continue for 30 years . . ." He said that "I don't think a country like the United States can commit itself to the extent it has and 'chicken out.' The consequence of getting out would be far more costly than the expense of staying in."

In 1969 Brzezinski shortened the new Thirty Year's War by 29 years and called for a cease-fire in Vietnam because he said, "most of the conditions justifying our original intervention now have been changed."

In the closing moments of a television interview in January of 1978, Brzezinski described the Vietnamese-Cambodian fighting as "the first case of a proxy war between China and the Soviet Union." When this judgment was challenged by other American foreign policy experts and State Department officials, Brzezinski hedged a little by observing that, "I think the Vietnamese-Cambodian conflicts have a reality of their own."

China

Somewhat peripheral to the major and continuing ideological and nuclear challenge and conflict (but bearing on it and influenced by it) were a number of other foreign policies, attitudes and actions conditioned by the major policy thrusts which consequently in greater or lesser degree kept foreign policy, if not outside history, certainly on the margin. First among these in magnitude and in importance was the China policy. For nearly 30 years following the 1949 fall of the Chiang Kai Shek government, we persisted in a policy of non-recognition and of continuing challenge and conflict with the communist government of China. Ironically, it was left to Richard Nixon, a longtime advocate of anti-Chinese policies, to move to give the United States' support to the admission of the People's Republic of China to the United Nations; and to Jimmy Carter, a succeeding president, to grant full diplomatic recognition. The non-recognition of China represents what seems to be a pattern for relationships with nations with which we have significant differences that can not be altered to our satisfaction, namely of refusing to recognize them for approximately 30 years. According to this formula, we may expect recognition of Cuba in 1991 or 1992, some 30 years after our disappointing invasion attempt in 1961, and recognition of the government of Vietnam early in the next century. It is reasonable to speculate on how the events in Vietnam, and even in Korea, might have been different if we had moved to some degree of recognition of China in the 1940s. For nearly 30 years, policy towards China was determined largely by the influence of what was labeled the China Lobby, made up of persons, generally anti-communist, sustained by others carrying a fear of the yellow horde, as reflected in Dean Rusk's warning in a statement made in support of the Vietnam War, or the likelihood that there would be one billion Chinese by the year 2000. (Just what bearing the fighting in Vietnam had on the year 2000, Rusk never quite made clear.) Robert McNamara's statement during debate on the production of antiballistic missiles was evidently meant to reassure the Russians and assure the anti-Chinese group that these missiles would be pointed, not at Russia, but at China.

The organization which most effectively opposed any opening or improvement of relationships with Communist China was the Committee of One Million Against the Admission of Communist China to the United Nations. The committee grew out of other earlier movements and organizations that made up parts of what came to be called early in the decade of the 1950s the China Lobby. Among its principal supporters were conservative organizations, labor leaders and unions (especially George Meany of the A.F.L.), and a wide spectrum of politicians, among them Congressman Walter Judd. He was sustained by other politicians, among them John Kennedy, who in a speech given in January of 1949 said that it was "of the utmost importance that we search out and spotlight those who must bear the responsibility for the disaster befalling China and the United States. Our diplomats and our President (then Harry Truman) have 'frittered away' what young Americans have fought to save," the congressman asserted. The one million signatures were obtained by July of 1954 and the Committee *for* One Million became the Committee *of* Several Million.

The committee remained an active force in influencing policy towards China for 18 years, achieving such successes or claimed successes as the defense of Quemoy and the Matsu islands in the Formosa Straits during the Eisenhower Administration; and the inclusion of planks opposing the admission of China to the United Nations in both the Republican and the Democratic Party platforms in 1956, as well as planks opposing relaxing of trade barriers between the United States and Communist China in 1957 and heading off efforts by organizations such as Americans for Democratic Action in their advocacy of negotiations towards admission of China to the United Nations. In 1961 President Kennedy, who as a candidate had opposed admission of China, agreed to a United Nations vote on the issue. The General Assembly subsequently voted 45 to 30 against the admission. Dean Rusk, as secretary of state under President Johnson, reassured the committee of the continuing opposition of that administration to any change in the United States-China relations, and in 1964 both the Republican and the Democratic Party platforms again contained planks ruling out any recognition of China in the United Nations.

The position of the China block was further fortified by a religious force, inspired primarily by Christian missionaries, former missionaries and their children. Most prominent among the former was Congressman Walter Judd who had been a medical missionary to

China, and among the latter, Henry Luce who was born in China to a missionary family in the field. Anti-Red China policy was also strongly supported by the Catholic hierarchy and missionary societies. The press generally supported the anti-China policy, but none more vigorously than Henry Luce of *Time* magazine, who according to Theodore White, a *Time* correspondent in China, would not print White's critical reports on the Chiang Kai Shek government and after giving White an increase in salary, limited his reporting in China to military matters. White accepted the limitation, but in his autobiography writes that he did not like doing so.

In addition to continuous opposition to recognition, the lobby also opposed trade with Mainland China. The Eisenhower government was severely critical of the British for relaxing their restriction on China trade and banned free travel of newspaper persons; in 1957 it denied Mrs. Franklin Roosevelt permission to travel in China to interview Chinese leaders. Grains sales to China were proscribed, even though other grain-growing nations like Canada and Australia were engaged in such trade. The restrictive policy was even more ridiculous in some instances; in 1961, following the imposition of an embargo on imports of sugar from Cuba, Congress was faced with the problem of reallocating quotas. In the course of the proceedings, it was proposed that a quota of 10,000 tons, approximately one boatload out of 2½ million tons available for distribution, be granted to Ireland. All seemed to be going well until a vigorous and thorough anti-communist member of Congress discovered that Ireland was importing sugar from Poland. The question was raised as to whether any of the communist-produced sugar would be transshipped to the United States. Upon the receipts of assurances that only sugar raised from the "old sod" would be sent to the United States, the 10,000 ton quota was approved.

With the election of Richard Nixon, the committee and its position seemed safe and secure. Nixon had been against Communist China throughout his political career. His actions in opening the door to China demonstrated the validity of a cynic's rule for voting for presidential candidates as follows: Pay no attention to what a candidate says that he or she will do, if it is something they can do in any case. Similarly, pay no attention to what he or she says he or she will not do, if it is something they couldn't do in any event. Take a careful look at what they say they will do, if it is something they might do. But look especially at what the candidates for the presidency say they won't do, if it is something they could do, and might do, especially if it is something the voter thinks is highly important.

President Nixon first relaxed trade and travel regulations, then in 1971 he visited China. The committee closed down on October 25, 1971, the day on which the United Nations General Assembly voted 76 to 35 to seat the People's Republic of China and to expel the Republic of China—the Nationalist Chinese government that had controlled only Formosa for over 20 years. The United States' diplomatic recognition of the Peking government as the government of China was to follow in the Carter Administration.

The Carter Administration demonstrated its anti-communism by keeping the United States athletes out of the 1980 Olympic games in Moscow because of the Russian invasion of Afghanistan and also placed an embargo on shipments of grain to Russia. In his campaign for the presidency in 1980, Ronald Reagan promised that if elected he would repeal the embargo on the sale of nine million tons of wheat and corn to Russia. On June 9, 1991, he lifted the embargo. About the same time the administration announced a plan to sell surplus butter to foreign countries—evidently in its original proposal including Russia among those countries, Alexander Haig, then the secretary of state, intervened and according to one unidentified White House source was "eloquent and convincing" in persuading the president to exclude Russia as a possible buyer. "No butter to the Russians" was the word; anything else would be "sending the wrong message" to the Soviets, top advisers to the president were reported to believe. The Russians, according to this view, could eat bread made from United States wheat, with oleo spread made from United States corn, but were to have no butter made from the cream of free world cows, contented or not. Evidently the use of butter is the break point between a free society and a totalitarian or authoritarian one, and Haig intended to hold the line, or maintain the spread.

CHAPTER III

Back into History

AND SO FOR SOME 40 YEARS THE NUCLEAR AND CONVENTIONAL ARMS race ran on with a series of covering concepts, all requiring more arms, especially of the nuclear type. The arms buildup continued until the meeting of President Reagan and Chairman Gorbachev in Iceland, at which meeting both national leaders agreed that each country had more than enough weapons to meet the threat the countries posed for each other and decided that the time for reason and proportion had arrived, and that the time had come to call off the disarmament experts, that is, the persons who were expert in measuring the relationships between conventional and non-conventional weapons, who could distinguish in quantitative degrees between strategic and nonstrategic nuclear weapons and weapon systems, who knew or pretended to know the rough equivalence of a cruise missile to a stealth bomber, etc.; and to retire permanently or temporarily the experts in geopolitics and real politics, who had laid upon modern international affairs the patterns of the Austro-Hungarian Empire and the balance of power theory and techniques of the Congress of Vienna.

All was changed, not just by moves by Gorbachev, but by admitting to realities that had been identifiable since the early 1970s, by which time it was clear that the concept of nuclear weapons as the sword, and conventional weapon systems as the shield, was no longer relevant, if it ever was, and that nuclear weapons had become the shield for both East and West, and that conventional weapons and forces were little more than a paper sword. Hungarians in the 1950s and Czechs in the 1960s had shown their will to resist Soviet domination, which should have led anyone Russian and who was counting on Warsaw Pact troops to the conclusion that Russia could not count on unquestioning loyalty from Warsaw Pact troops in a military move against the West, unless the target of that movement was German forces and power. With the deployment of tactical, field and nuclear weapons in Europe, together with the excessive supplies of strategic nuclear weapons held by both Russia and the United States, the possibility of a Russian invasion of Europe was practically nil. The continued presence of United States troops and military power in Europe from that point on was justified as much by anticipation of a German military buildup, either by Germany acting directly or with justification because of a reduction of United States' forces in Europe, as it was justified by a Russian threat, real or imagined. The United States troops were, in fact, double hostages, to both East and West, possibly triple hostages, if one includes Germans who were and (one can assume) are opposed to German rearmament. The United States might have in fairness asked the Russians to make a contribution to the support of the United States forces in Germany, as insurance against Germany, since we were asking Germany to contribute to the support of troops as insurance against the Russians.

What are the realities today?

1. The likelihood of a Russian-American military conflict is by any reasonable judgment nonexistent.
2. The Warsaw Pact military forces are no threat to either the West or the East. They are at best and at worse forces bearing on the internal stability or instability of their respective countries, which may be moved to invite intervention from either East or West, or both, to stabilize internal conditions.
3. The withdrawal of Russian troops from the Eastern European countries is a fact which is all but complete.
4. The reunification of Germany has been accomplished.
5. NATO is not yet an anachronism, but must certainly be looked at for restructuring and a redefinition of purpose. The essence of the situation was made clear during a recent visit of Admiral Groves to Russia, when a Russian general asked Groves, "Why don't we have joint maneuvers?" Groves was at a loss to suggest whom the maneuvers might have as a potential enemy. The Russian did not supply an answer.

A nonaggression treaty among European nations, including Russia and the United States, could formalize historical realities. Withdrawal or significant reduction of United States forces in Europe would be a proper subject to take up at that time.

The time has come to include Russia in the financial and trading complex of the non-communist world, and for the United States to at least open negotiations on recognizing Cuba and Vietnam. It should be recognized that what we now have in Europe is a delayed ending of World War II. A plan comparable to the Marshall Plan is in order to help the nations of Central Europe and Russia, with Japan and Germany bearing the major financial burden of that reconstruction, and beyond that, positive reconstruction.

For the first time in over 40 years, nearly a half century, Russia and the United States are moving into a political, economic and cultural relationship, not the same as that which existed before the Russian Revolution of 1918, and not the same as that which seemed likely after the end of World War II, but one which gives promise of understanding and cooperation between the two nations. Such understanding and cooperation, if it is established and if it grows, can have great bearing on order and progress in the world during the next half century, which is about as far as prudent observers of world affairs should project their judgments and prophecies.

The famous photograph of soldiers, American and Russian, joining hands as they met after common victory over Nazi Germany was the last real evidence of the participation of the two nations in a common history.

Since that time, ideological differences, misunderstandings, personalities, mistakes of judgment, and accidents of history have kept the two nations apart.

Intemperate language made its contribution to continuing division: The Cold War was neither cold nor a war; The Iron Curtain was a rhetorical flourish that took on substance; Containment is a descriptive word intended for limited application, which was made into a doctrine. Covert action by both the KGB and the CIA took on a life of its own. Misinformation and propaganda became accepted instruments of conflict.

Opportunities for improved relationships and relaxation of tensions came and went, sometimes because of actions or lack of action by one nation or the other: The closing of access to Berlin by Russia and U2 overflights by the United States. These and other less defined events clouded and interfered with the chances of improved relationships during President Eisenhower's years in the White House, when it was believed that understanding and trust demonstrated between Russian and United States military leaders would carry over into the politics of the post war period. Then followed the building of the Berlin Wall by Russia, the invasion of Cuba by the United States, the most serious confrontation, the Missile Crisis, and the consequent loss of the opportunity for changed political and economic relationships, which the Khrushchev chairmanship promised. Since then we have experienced some 20 years of nuclear and other military competitions or diplomatic contests, of limited cultural exchange, and of the politicization of sports. Each country developed doctrines to fit its purposes, most notably the Eisenhower doctrine for the Middle East and later the Breshnev doctrine for Central Asia. Each country used ideology to justify and sustain its actions, the United States for the Vietnam War and Russia in the Afghanistan conflict.

We now have a third opportunity to move to improved relationships and understanding. A more significant beginning, actually much more than a beginning, has been made in the agreements followed by action to reduce and limit operative nuclear weapons. There is a promise of more progress.

Trade relationships have been slightly improved. The prospects are for greater advances. Actions such as those taken in the 1950s to prevent the building of American automobile and tire factories in Russia and the later embargo on grain shipments imposed during the Carter Administration, barring unforeseen developments, are not in prospect.

During four decades cultural exchanges have been limited and irregular, often more propaganda devices than free and open cultural events.

Improved political and economic relationships will mean little and be highly unstable unless sustained by continuing free cultural exchanges. We need not and cannot wait for perfect understanding and agreement; such conditions do not exist among nations of Western Europe and the United States. But nations that honor and revere writers like Chekhov and Gorky, Dostoevsky and Tolstoy, and modern poets and novelists like Pasternak, Voznesenski and Yevtushenko as the United States does; and nations that read our writers, like Faulkner, Whitman, London and Vonnegut, as Russia does, should be able to find common political ground, and resolve differences or set them aside with the same spirit that Tolstoy showed toward Gorky when he wrote, "Gorky has something to say. He exaggerates, untruthfully, but he loves, and we recognize our brothers where we have not seen them before."

The Persian Gulf War

Involvement in the Persian Gulf War is of another order than were the conflicts the United States has been involved in in the last half century. Ideological distinctions that have marked, and in part determined our policies in Europe, in South and Central America, in Africa and in the Far East are not applicable. The communists are not there or coming. We were not invited in because of external or internal threats of communist takeovers. There were no covering treaties in place, no anticipatory resolutions of the stature of the Eisenhower Middle East resolution or the Tonkin Gulf resolution. The doctrine of presidential continuity did not apply.

For months, even years, before the hostilities between the United States and Iraq broke out, we were maintaining certainly not an unfriendly relationship, if not a friendly one, involving diplomacy, economic and military relationships, sufficient it appears to lead Saddam Hussein to think that he could move against Kuwait without fear of our intervening. April Glaspie, our ambassador to Iraq in the months preceding the invasion, in testifying before a congressional committee, explained that Saddam had misunderstood U.S. intentions and that the State Department persons who were watching him did not foresee what he would do because he was "dumber" than they thought him to be. This explanation introduced a new factor for judging foreign policy errors. Ms. Glaspie did not explain whether the misjudgment occurred because State Department personnel were not smart enough to note the "dumbness" of Saddam or whether they were so smart that they could not reach far enough down in the scale of intelligence to contemplate dumbness on the Saddam level.

It was not the invasion of Kuwait that moved the United States into action, but the belief that Saudi Arabia was in danger of invasion also, with the consequent possibility that all Arabian oil would be controlled by Saddam Hussein. Such control would have certainly threatened supplies of oil to the United States, to Japan and to other nations of the world. In keeping with our national obligations to protect lifelines to vital resources, intervention was called for and justifiable. Almost immediately, additional more comprehensive reasons and objectives for intervention were introduced, progressively involving the interests and obligations of other nations as primary, and the obligation of the United States as secondary or supportive. The liberation of Kuwait was declared as a purpose scarcely separable from our defense of Saudi Arabia and its oil. The liberation of Kuwait was of interest to the Arab states as a sign to Saddam that territorial lines were to be preserved. It was of concern also to oil interests of other countries, especially to the British, also because of their interest in protecting the integrity of their mapmaking. Similarly the added purpose of destroying or weakening Saddam's military forces was of interest to the Arab nations and to Israel as was the objective of destroying Iraq's chemical and germ warfare stocks and facilities and its potential to produce nuclear weapons. The reasons given by President Bush and by Secretary Baker—to protect our way of life, to ensure jobs, and to take a major step towards establishing a new world order—were added entries. This escalation of purpose and objectives is comparable to the escalation of purpose and objectives as the military forces in Vietnam were increased: from helping the French put down a colonial revolt to helping anti-communist forces in a civil war in the South, to repelling an invasion from the North, to stopping the expansion of communism, to protecting the security of the Free World.

The Persian Gulf operation demonstrated our potential to deploy troops and materials. It was an amazing logistical achievement, even though unobstructed by enemy forces and with an assured place for landing troops and supplies and with a fuel supply in place. The invasion was accompanied by masterful diplomatic achievements in getting support from the United Nations Security Council, the United Nations itself and from most of the Arab nations. The action was supported not only by the opinion of decent mankind, but by some nations whose opinions on the record fall a little short of decency.

The war has been declared over and its mission accomplished and victory celebrations and parades have been held. The Washington victory celebration of the Persian Gulf War, otherwise and officially known as Desert Storm, may have established a precedent for greater, or lesser, or comparable military victory celebrations in the future. If it has, although new to the United States, it would not be new to history. In most major elements it followed closely the triumphal celebrations of the Roman Republic, and of the subsequent imperial period.

In its early years, the triumph noted the return of the king and his army from a victorious military campaign. The ceremony included an offering of thanksgiving to the god or the state and rites designed and directed at purification of the top general and his troops. The purgative element was dropped in later triumphs. It was customary during the years of the republic to hail the returning general as imperator. In the imperial period, the honor of triumph was reserved for the emperor and his family. President Bush did not wholly displace General Schwarzkopf, but shared billing with him. Whereas General Schwarzkopf was not hailed as imperator, he was hailed by some as a possible presidential or vice presidential candidate of either the Republican or the Democratic Party. Returning General Colin Powell was given similar mention.

In the Roman triumph, as in the Washington one, the victorious general praised his soldiers collectively and in special cases individually, and bestowed honors and decorations on the deserving. The dead were commemorated.

According to Roman practice, a large amount of booty was distributed among the soldiers who had served and especially among leading generals and officers. Leading generals in the Persian Gulf War were not rewarded handsomely by the United States government, but by the private sector, especially by the corporate business community and most notably by those that are a part of the military-industrial complex, through lecture fees (as much as eighty thousand dollars per speech for some speeches, according to booking agents), by being hired as consultants, by being placed on boards of directors of corporations and, in some cases, being made officers of companies.

Lesser officers and rank and file personnel were rewarded with special benefits, some from the U.S. Congress, with strong support from those members who voted in favor of delaying military action until after economic and other sanctions had been tried, some from state and local governments, from airlines, hotels and other business and service entities.

The processions in the Roman triumphs were most popular with the populace. The procession was generally lead by public officials, followed by trumpeters, spoils of victory, paintings or models of conquered countries or cities, slogans on tablets, the most famous surviving one being the "veni, vidi, vici" of Caesar after his triumph over Pontus. Captured arms were displayed as well as hostages and prisoners in chains. The general did not stand alone in his chariot, but was surrounded by family and relatives. After the procession, the chief capitves were killed—in the early years of the triumphs by being beheaded, but in later more humane times by being hanged.

The parade of victory following Desert Storm did not quite match the processions of the Roman triumphs, but it came close. The generals were there with families nearby. The troops and the armor were there. There was music, trumpets, banners. Soldiers of past wars who had not returned to triumphs were included. Booty was not on display, an element which might have been represented by including a fleet of oil and gas trucks. Captives were not displayed, but Noriega, as our most important captive of recent wars, might have been included. The chairman of the Republican Party in advance of the parade declared that members of Congress who had not supported the resolution giving the president unconditional powers to take military action were, or are, to be held hostage politically for their vote. There were no executions at the end of the ceremonies, although Mrs. Bush was reported during the war as saying of Saddam Hussein: "I would like to see him hung." (*The Washington Post* headline changed the "hung" to "hanged.")

There are a few lessons we might learn from the study of the history of the Roman triumphs. First is the danger of proliferation. In the 150 years between 220 B.C. and 70 B.C., some 100 trimphs were held to edify and delight the Roman citizens and to distract them from worrying about the continuing disintegration and decline of the republic. In this spirit we might have celebrated the victory in Grenada and that in Panama as triumphs, or possibly done what Senator Aiken proposed we do about the war in Vietnam, namely declare the war won and celebrate a victory.

The Romans, moved by the increasing number of triumphs, adopted tighter rules. By the first century B.C., a condition to having the celebration was that a foreign enemy had been defeated in a "just war." Under this standard the invasion of Panama might have qualified as it was labeled "Operation Just Cause" by the Bush Administration. It might not have qualified under another first century requirement that there could be no celebration unless at least 5000 enemies had been killed, not counting slaves, or civilians, and especially not children. The generals to be honored had to affirm the count under oath. The Romans for a time also imposed a requirement that before the victory celebration could be held, the war had to have ended, and the army that had fought returned so that it could take part in the ceremony. This requirement was subsequently modified. As the Roman general might say of the Persian Gulf War: "veni, vidi, vici, reliqui."

Forward or Backward to Unreality

The Bush Administration did not long remain in the reality of history opened to us by the changes in Russia. The Secretary of Defense warned of the unreliability of communists in the past. The president expressed reluctance to provide economic assistance beyond advice and counsel until Russia had proved itself more fully as a society in which individual and political rights were more perfectly demonstrated, and Russia had proved itself ready for the New World Order.

President Bush in January said that no cost would be too high for the liberation of Kuwait. More sober estimates of the potential cost of victory were offered by Dr. John Pasatore, a member of the medical faculty at Tufts University and secretary of International Physicians for the Prevention of Nuclear War, when he told a House Committee on January 15, 1991, that casualties among United States soldiers could reach 45,000 with 10,000 dead. The organization said that 60,000 body bags would be shipped to the Middle East. The army was reported in February as having 6000 medical personnel. Brigadier General Blanck of the Army Surgeon General's office said in February, ". . . due to high concentrations of armored troops and artillery, there will be blast injuries, high-velocity missile wounds, shrapnel wounds and burns." Early estimates of 20,000 injuries and deaths were discounted. Blanck said, "We're planning for worse than that, but given the success of our air strikes in Iraq, I don't expect it."

General Blanck said as reported on February 1 that well over 20,000 medical technicians and other medical personnel, including doctors and nurses, were in the Gulf area. No firm estimates of what President Bush was willing to spend on the war were offered. Important questions were left unanswered, if they were ever asked of the administration, questions that should have been faced by the Administration before or while committing 500,000 military personnel with supporting equipment to a war we were certain to win,

and in which casualties in great numbers were to be inflicted on the
enemy.

1. Why was the advice of military experts or of those reputed to
    be experts, such as former Secretary of Defense Robert McNa-
    mara and retired Admiral Crowe, ignored?

2. Why were the military forces (most of them armed with Ameri-
    can weapons) of the Arab nations aligned against Iraq, not
    asked, urged or assisted to assume the major military responsi-
    bilities in the prospective war? These nations have a total com-
    bined population of approximately 100 million persons against
    an Iraqi population of approximately 12 million. Egypt has an
    army strong enough to have fought the Israelis in 1973; Iran has
    armed forces which held Iraq to something approaching a draw
    in the recent war between those two nations. The Saudis and
    the small oil-producing countries have advanced U.S. equip-
    ment; the Syrians are engaged almost continuously in military
    actions in Lebanon.

3. What is the New World Order to be established, as some aides
    have hinted? It is a version of the "Pax America" the Pentagon
    was interested in back in the 1960s? How is this world order to
    be maintained?

4. Why has the United States not taken the initiative in setting up
    a conference on the general problems of the Middle East, or
    indicated a willingness to follow the initiatives of others, espe-
    cially since the changes in Russia and the possibility of construc-
    tive participation by the Russians greatly increase the chances of
    success in efforts to establish order and peace in the area?

5. Why is no effort being made now to establish an energy pro-
    gram for the United States?

6. Why are efforts to make the Middle East a nuclear-free area,
    as part of a more comprehensive nuclear non-proliferation and
    nuclear disarmament effort, seemingly on hold, if under any
    consideration?

7. With chemical and germ warfare a possibility in the Middle
    East, why is there no significant effort, or disposition in evi-
    dence, on the part of the United States to move toward interna-
    tional banning of such weapons, including our own neutron
    bombs?

8. What was the purpose of U.S. support of the administration of
    Saddam Hussein during the Iraq War against Iran? What part

did the United States take in selling arms to Iran in the Iran-Contra affair?

9. Why is not a world conference or United Nations action proposed to reexamine the 1923 mapping principally by British politicians of the Middle East, especially since those maps bear on the Kuwait-Iraq conflict?

10. Why were the Israelis kept from defending their own country when under Scud attack and listed for destruction by Saddam, whose efforts were supported by Jordan, and not permitted to bomb plants producing chemical and biological weapons and potential nuclear weapons, thus establishing some claim to recognition by Arab countries, whose safety and security were advanced by the Israel actions? Even now it is not too late to have Muslim countries occupy Iraq.

No recent war has been brought to a reasonably good conclusion without occupation. Not the war with Japan or the war with Germany or the Korean War. The hurried withdrawal of U.S. forces sustained de Tocqueville's observation that such action is an unhappy mark of democracies. Of equal seriousness is the presidential disposition to avoid responsibility until success is achieved.

Rejection of presidential responsibility for war and other actions and decisions is not a Bush innovation. Lyndon Johnson sought the protection of the Tonkin Gulf resolution and noted that he was only carrying out what three presidents before him had progressively supported in Vietnam. Richard Nixon noted that he was carrying forward, even into Cambodia, what four of his predecessors had sustained, and called the war a democratic war. Ronald Reagan took credit for the Grenada action, first billed as an incursion and then as an invasion. There is no verb "incurse." But Reagan passed off the deaths of marines in Lebanon as a kind of happening. President Carter attributed failures during his administration to the malaise that affected the nation.

This gradual rejection of presidential responsibility is coming to full term, possibly reaching institutional status in the Bush Administration, which may be the first fully no fault presidency in our history.

As the war was developing and in the early stages of engagement, President Bush said he was going to follow the advice of the military. In fact, he did not heed Colin Powell's advice to delay the beginning of hostilities, or those of General Schwarzkopf to continue the pursuit and destruction of Saddam's army.

The deaths and destruction resulted from the early action in the liberation of Kuwait, and the attacks on Saddam's forces were all, the president said, attributable to Saddam and on his conscience. The shelling and bombing of troops, tanks and trucks, etc., during the retreat of the Iraqi forces, were justified, according to administration spokespersons, as allowed under a Geneva Convention. The forces had not surrendered, but were assumed to be moving to a new position from which they would resume hostilities.

The most recent assertion of lack of war-related responsibility of President Bush took place in a Houston, Texas, church on Sunday, April 7, when the president absolved himself, and by extension the people of the United States, of any responsibility for the condition of various Iraqi rebel and refugee groups. Whereas it is acknowledged that President Bush did encourage revolt against Saddam, he did not, he asserted, promise potential rebels any support, armed or otherwise. Moreover, the administration has noted that any such assistance would be intervention in the internal affairs of another nation, an action not allowed by the United Nations. Had the United Nations been in existence during World War II, and had Hitler (Bush called Saddam another Hitler) promised to give up conquered territory, suspend production of weapons of mass destruction, and make reparations, he might then have been allowed to go on as long as he executed only German Jews.

In other areas of political and governmental actions, the president has demonstrated the same disposition to avoid or deny personal or presidential responsibility.

The budget deficit he blames on the Democratic Congress. He might have gone farther and blamed it on the American electorate, since that electorate chose a Democratic Congress in 1990 despite the president's drive for the election of Republicans. He has taken no responsibility for the savings and loan difficulties, even though he might have learned of it from his son, and has shown little concern for it or for related difficulties in the banking community and in Housing and Urban Development.

Although other presidents and presidential candidates were held responsible for their vice presidents or running mates (Franklin Roosevelt rejected vice presidents as future running mates. Eisenhower answered for Richard Nixon in 1952; McGovern was held responsible for his choice and then rejection of Tom Eagleton.

Nixon, belatedly, had to take blame for his choice of Spiro Agnew and Mondale for Geraldine Ferraro), Bush treats the Quayle vice presidency as though it were an accident or an act of nature, as if it were something he found in the office one morning. Although he supported the war in Vietnam, he avoids defending that support, but talks of "kicking the Vietnam Syndrome" (an action hard to visualize) and saying that he would not do it again, or that if he did, he would do it differently.

What seems to be indifference to responsibilities, or an amoral attitude towards such responsibilities, is indicated in Bush's personal behavior and language. The vacation taken by the President in the early stages of the Gulf War was defended on the grounds that the president was not "re-creating," but something different, pronounced "rek-creating." The president recommended the same indulgence for all the citizens. In the midst of a critical press conference, or a press conference on a critical matter such as the one he gave from a golf cart as the war was intensifying, he interrupts or terminates the conference by saying, "gotta go now . . ." or casually makes statements about most serious matters without taking his hands out of his pants pockets.

The president's holiday fishing vacation in Florida at Easter, taken as post-Desert Storm conditions were worsening, was taken not on the president's initiative, but because Barbara insisted that he go, a White House spokesperson said, and added that the fishing for bonefish would be for the president "rejuvenative." One can understand why a tired president might wish to be restored to his normal level of adult energy and responsiveness, but why he or his aides would want him youthful requires some explanation.

Peggy Noonan, in her book about the Reagan Administration *What I Saw at the Revolution,* makes several observations about George Bush which help to explain his detachment or flight from responsibility. According to Ms. Noonan, who did some speech writing for candidate Bush, he hated to say "I." If she wrote an "I" in a speech for him, he would, she writes, drop the phrase containing the pronoun, or drop a whole sentence rather than use the personal pronoun. She accommodated her writing to him. Instead of writing "I moved to Texas," she would write "moved to Texas." Instead of "We joined the Republican Party," she wrote "joined the Republican Party." And, she writes she imagined him at his oath-taking at the presidential inaugural not saying "I solemnly swear," by uttering phrases like "solemnly swear" and "will preserve and protect." The pronoun "we" was more acceptable to him, possibly because it denotes shared responsibility, in the manner noted by Mark Twain who said that no one should use the collective "we" excepting the king (or queen) of England, the archbishop of Canterbury (or Pope, one can assume) or someone with a tapeworm. Ms. Noonan suggests that this disposition to avoid the use of the pronoun "I" had its beginning with his stern mother's admonishing him when he was a boy to not use it.

This may be true, but whatever its origin, the inclination could very well have been nurtured by three of the political offices held by Bush prior to his election to the presidency. First, his chairmanship of the Republican Party, an office (one can say the same of the chairmanship of the Democratic Party) not recommended for character building. George Bush accomplished little during his tour in that office, neither did he define nor redefine the function of that office. The best evidence of how he looked on the office and its operations is in his proposal that William Bennet become chairman of the Republican Party, and following Bennet's refusal, his recommendation of Lee Atwater.

The second office held by Bush, which might have blunted his sense of personal responsibility and sensitivity to frankness and openness in conduct, was his service as director of the Central Intelligence Agency. And the third was his eight years of service as vice president. He entered that office after having denounced Reagan's "voodoo economics" and emerged as a most enthusiastic and dedicated convert and advocate.

Well, as President Bush might say at this point: "Gotta go now. . . ." Where—but backward or forward to unreality.

PART II

CHAPTER IV

Borders

A SECOND MARK OF A COUNTRY'S COLONIAL DEPENDENCE IS LACK OF control over its own borders, either as defined and mapped, with mother countries, international agencies or other outside authorities changing the lines, or abolishing them; or, if the lines are firm, lack of control over who or what crosses those borders. Thus Pope Alexander VI decreed in 1493, in what became known as the "papal line of demarcation," that lands and peoples east of a line drawn from the North Pole to the South Pole 100 leagues west of the Cape Verde Islands were reserved to colonization by the Portuguese, while lands and peoples west of that line were reserved for Spanish colonization and exploitation.

In subsequent decades and centuries, additional colonial claims were made by other countries in the Americas, in the Middle East, in Africa, in the Far East, etc. Claims were disputed, sometimes adjusted after minor wars, sometimes after major wars, by purchase and by other means with the colonies in most cases having little to say about the new arrangements and definitions of territories.

Of all the colonizing countries, the British were the most resourceful. They picked up colonial properties by conquest of indigenous or established peoples, as in the case of the Irish and of the Boers; in settlement of war, as in the case of Canada; by default, as in the Falklands and Australia; through private ventures, like those of Rhodes in Africa and Clive in India; and more or less by accident.

The definition of the borders of the United States began in colonial times, especially following the defeat of the French in the French and Indian Wars, and was further advanced through the Louisiana

Purchase in 1803, the annexation of Florida, the purchase and military conquest of Mexican territories, and finally with the purchase of Alaska from the Russians. Despite the "fifty-four forty or fight" slogan and the threat of war with Britain over our northern border, diplomacy prevailed and the 1846 agreement set the United States-Canadian border at the 49th parallel. There has been no change in these borders since they were settled in the last century, except for a minor concession during the Johnson Administration to Mexican claims to a small piece of land that had been separated from Mexico by the meandering of the Rio Grande River.

Illegal transportation of goods across United States borders and illegal entry of persons have been matters of some concern and controversy, beginning in colonial times. Then the concern was more over what might be shipped out rather than what might be brought in, and over what kinds of immigrants might be allowed in rather than over number of immigrants.

Deterrents to immigration were the dangers; natural and human, Indians and French in the case of English settlers, Indians and English in the case of others. The cost of passage and hardships of voyages also discouraged possible settlers. An accepted estimate is that by 1640 the population of the colonies was about 25,000. By the year 1776 the population of the colonies was approximately two-and-a-half million persons. Nearly all were of European stock—English, French, German, Dutch, Spanish and Portuguese. Many came for economic reasons. Many others came for religious purposes to avoid persecution at home and to find religious freedom, at least for themselves, in the new land, reserving in some cases the right to exclude and discriminate against persons of other sects, if not to persecute them. Quakers settled in Pennsylvania, Catholics in Maryland. Restrictive legislation and attitudes discouraged immigration in a number of colonies. This was true especially in the case of immigrants who were labeled paupers and criminals.

Among those who came or were brought to the colonies involuntarily were children kidnapped from English slums and sold as labor to Americans. English judges sent both vagrants and felons to the colonies as punishment. Southern colonies, Georgia especially, were recipients of criminals sent by the English courts. It is estimated that 50,000 persons were sent to the Southern colonies under penal sanctions in the 50 years preceding the American Revolution.

The colonies generally were unable to check unwanted immigration by legislation and by enforcement of laws because they lacked central and accepted authority.

Meanwhile, the importation of slaves continued, primarily by the English who had been given a virtual monopoly over the slave trade by the Treaty of Utrecht in 1713.

Colonial

Colonial attitudes toward immigration persisted after the Revolution. Quality of immigrants, rather than numbers, was the continuing concern. No extensive Federal legislation dealing with immigration was enacted for many years. There were two principal reasons for this delay. First, for almost 100 years it was not settled as to whether the federal government had power under the constitution to regulate immigration; and second, because national interest and policy through these same years favored unrestricted immigration. Immigration just happened during this period.

Under the Articles of Confederation, there was no declaration of governmental power over immigration. There was confusion over statutes adopted during the colonial period, but each state was allowed to determine its own immigration policy.

Although the United States Constitution adopted in 1789 granted Congress broad power to regulate foreign commerce, it was not clear that foreign commerce included immigration. Not until nearly 100 years later it was established by the Supreme Court in *Henderson vs. New York* that state restrictions on immigration were unconstitutional and an infringement on federal power over foreign commerce.

During this near century of uncertainty Congress did not attempt to regulate immigration, but did pass a series of acts regulating naturalization and defining citizenship. The first such act, passed in 1790, granted citizenship to immigrants (the constitutional ban on an immigrant becoming president of the United States was unchallenged). Subsequent legislation required longer periods of residency and renunciation of foreign allegiances and of titles of nobility. The first quality control act was enacted in 1798. It authorized the president to deport dangerous aliens. The act expired in two years and was not renewed. In 1802 a new naturalization act extended to five years the residency requirement for citizenship. (Touching on immigration were a series of passenger acts in 1819, 1847, 1848 and 1855, setting space and food standards for ocean transports.)

No official records of immigration were kept until 1820. It is estimated that about 250,000 immigrants came to the United States between 1790 and 1820. In the years from 1820 to 1880, while the issue of immigration was debated without concomitant legislation, ten million immigrants entered the United States.

Discontent with the open immigration policy grew as the number of immigrants increased and as the cultural character of the immigrants changed. Between 1820 and 1880, because of political abuse by the English accompanied by economic disorder, especially the failure of potato crops, over 2.8 million Irish came to the United States. German Catholics came in large numbers during the European depressions of the 1840s.

These Catholic immigrants were not well received by American Protestants. The anti-Catholicism of colonial days resurfaced under the leadership of Protestant evangelicals, Nativists, the Order of the Star Spangled Banner, the Know Nothing Party and social reformers. Generally these persons and organizations campaigned for legislation limiting, if not halting, immigration of religiously undesirable persons, and also prohibiting naturalized citizens with the wrong religious backgrounds from participating in the nation's political actions.

This same attitude persists today and manifests itself in proposals for constitutional amendments to declare the United States to be a Christian nation and in legislation to require non-Christians to take a different oath of loyalty on the presumption that their oaths to a Christian god are not valid.

The worried groups were somewhat successful at the state level, as they are today especially at the school board level, but were unsuccessful at the Federal level, in part because politicians at the national level sought the vote of old and new immigrants. In Andrew Jackson's presidential campaign of 1832, campaign material was printed in German to attract the votes of German-Americans.

During the Civil War, the need for labor moved the country, both North and South, to encourage immigration. An 1864 Act validated contracts in which future wages could be pledged to pay for ocean passage. After the Civil War, federal law became more restrictive and assertive. The Act of 1864, which had encouraged immigration, was repealed in 1868 and in 1875 the first Federal restrictive act was passed. The restrictions were not quantitative but qualitative. Borrowing from colonial legislation, the Federal statute of 1875 banned convicts and prostitutes. The act also dealt with new problems in the Western states, in which expansion required large numbers of workers in the mines and in building the railroads. Tension developed between native workers and immigrant workers of European and Oriental origins.

Chinese workers, imported as early as 1850, refused to be assimilated and also worked for lower wages. Congress enacted laws banning "coolie labor" contracts and immigration of persons for lewd and immoral purposes. When Chinese continued to immigrate voluntarily or came in through Canada, Congress passed in 1882 the Chinese Exclusion Act, the first racist restrictive act, although the act had cultural implications. The act suspended all immigration of Chinese laborers for ten years and forbade any court to admit Chinese to citizenship. The act was extended in 1902 and subsequently made permanent, remaining on the statute books until repealed in 1943. The 1882 Act added to the list of exclusions, including along with the convicts and prostitutes lunatics, idiots and those "likely to become public charges." It also imposed a head tax on arriving immigrants, ostensibly to raise money to meet administrative expenses. It also had the effect of discouraging the poor of other nations from being added to the relief rolls. In subsequent laws, the original 50-cent fee was raised to two dollars, a substantial charge at the time. Health criteria were also established by which immigrants were rejected and sent back home for such widely prevalent illnesses as tuberculosis and trachoma, an eye infection.

Despite restrictions and obstacles, over 5.2 million immigrants arrived in the decade of the 1880s. As immigration came to be looked upon as a threat to the United States economy and society, Congress responded by adding the diseased, paupers and polygamists to the lists of those to be excluded. It also forbade advertisements in foreign countries designed to encourage or assist immigration to America. Medical examinations were required. Immigration declined by 1.5 million in the 1890s to 3.7 million, in contrast with the 5.2 million of the previous decade.

When immigration numbers began to rise in the first decade of the next century, Congress moved in 1903 to pass new laws excluding epileptics, the insane, beggars and anarchists. The last was the first move to exclude persons because of political views. In 1907, the feebleminded, the tubercular and persons with mental or physical defects which "may affect" their ability to earn a living were added to the list.

In the same period, Japanese immigration was restricted by agreement between the United States and Japan. The new controls were not very effective, largely because they were difficult to administer and because of the limited amounts of money and the number of persons employed by the Bureau of Immigration and Naturalization. Nearly 8.8 million immigrants were admitted in the first decade of the 20th century.

Of more concern to Congress and the country than the large numbers were the types of persons coming into the United States. Whereas in the 1880s most immigrants came from northern and western Europe, in the years from 1900 to 1920 71 percent came from southern and eastern Europe, principally Latins, Slavs and Jews, all of whom were considered inferior and threatening to the predominant Anglo-Saxon population. Many of these new immigrants were slow to assimilate and, like the Chinese, settled into urban ethnic ghettos.

Literacy was next introduced as a control device. After a series of inquiries and commission studies, Congress concluded early in the 20th century that a liberal immigration policy was no longer beneficial to the country and passed laws imposing a literacy test. The 1917 Act, passed over the veto of President Wilson, was designed to limit immigration from southern and eastern Europe by barring those persons who were unable to read some language. A move to exclude blacks was defeated but the immigration head tax was raised to eight dollars. The act also prohibited immigration of Asians within defined latitudes and longitudes. In a 1918 act, the definition of "anarchists" was changed to give it wider applicability. By 1920, almost every limiting condition had been applied: cultural, including literacy, racial, physical, moral and mental condition; geographical definitions, political views and admission taxes, a kind of means test.

The 1920s was to see the introduction of quotas. In the years following World War I, efforts at controlling immigration shifted from quality requirements to numerical quotas. This was a major shift in the approach of the United States to immigration controls. In the 1921 law, immigration from any nation was limited to three percent of the number of foreign-born persons of that nationality residing in the United States as of the 1910 census. The total quota allowed was 357,000. Because a few foreign-born persons from the south and east of Europe lived in the United States in 1910, that region's quota was 45,000 less than that allowed for northern and western Europe. Provisions in the law permitting certain non quota exceptions allowed restricted groups to enter. Thus the law permitted a person to be admitted to the United States if that person had lived in a Western Hemisphere country for one year. This was later changed to five years. The effect of the law was to quantify, depersonalize and derationalize immigration policy.

In 1924, immigration was further reduced by a change in the law which reduced the three percent of those residing in the United States in 1910 to two percent of the foreign-born residing in the United States in 1890. This formula reduced the total quota to a little more than 164,000 and made the southern and eastern European quotas even smaller than they had been under the 1910 Act.

Despite the limiting terms of the 1924 Act, immigration from southern and eastern countries of Europe equalled that from the preferred northern and western countries. A provision in the act exempting spouses of U.S. citizens from the quota limitations was used to circumvent the limitation of the law. Sham marriages became a common way of gaining admission to the United States. Marital fraud was accompanied by illegal border crossings. Immigration from within the Western Hemisphere began to increase in the 1920s, presenting new problems of border control. The Border Patrol was established in 1924. Total immigration in the years 1924–29 was estimated at 1.5 million. In 1929 a new quota base came into effect. It used the ethnic background of the whole U.S. population, rather than first generation population, as a base for establishing new quotas. Since the whole population of the United States was predominantly Anglo-Saxon, the new quota restricted immigration from the southern and eastern countries even more severely than had the previous quotas.

The Depression which began in 1929 and ran on until the beginning of World War II proved a greater deterrent to immigration than laws and limitations. Only half-a-million persons entered the country as immigrants in the 1930s.

Wartime need for workers and political considerations brought about two changes substantially different from previous standards and guides for admitting foreigners. The United States negotiated a temporary worker program with Mexico, and Congress, because of a wartime alliance with China, repealed the ban on Chinese immigration and established a quota of 105 Chinese per year; it also permitted Chinese immigrants to become naturalized citizens of the United States. After the war quota laws were further relaxed to accommodate refugees from Europe. President Truman in 1945 issued a directive to allow 40,000 war refugees to enter the United States. This was the first significant departure from previous policies of controlling immigration by regulation and by formula. The War Brides Act of 1945 and Fiancees Act of 1946 allowed about 123,000 wives, children and fiancees of WW II military personnel to enter the United States and the Displaced Persons Act of 1948 admitted another 400,000 refugees from Austria, Germany and Italy to the United States, although these admissions were counted against future quotas.

In 1953 the Refugee Relief Act allowed entrance of an additional 214,000 refugees. Similar measures were passed in 1956 and in 1957 to facilitate the entry of Hungarians and others fleeing communism as well as some persons from countries of the Middle East. The 1960 Refugee Act, known as the Fair Share Law, dealt with refugees and displaced persons in camps under the mandate of the United Nations high commissioner for refugees. The most significant changes in immigration policy were incorporated in the 1965 law.

The Immigration Act of 1965 was passed the same year this country instituted sweeping civil rights reforms. One hundred years after the Civil War, the country had finally evolved to the point where de jure discrimination against black citizens could no longer be tolerated. Amidst this climate of change and self-criticism for long-standing injustices, Congress also turned its attention to a policy that discriminated against people outside the United States. Prior to 1965, our immigration policies overtly favored immigrants from northern and western Europe and excluded, either in statute or practice, most other nationalities. Changing these discriminatory immigration policies had been a priority of President Kennedy, and like many other aspects of Lyndon Johnson's Great Society, the Immigration Act of 1965 became sort of a legislative tribute to our slain leader. Given the political tenor of the times, the debate focused more on the evils of the old system than on the virtues of the new. The new measure sought to destroy the objectionable features of the old law.

The 1965 changes to the immigration laws discounted the human factors that ultimately resulted in effects no one had anticipated. Congress in 1965 believed that it could institute immigration policies that gave hundreds of millions of people all over the world the hope of coming to the United States and still maintain control of the numbers. In the years since the law was passed, rapidly growing populations and increasing despair in many Third World countries have taken on a dynamic energy of their own that has wrested control of the United States immigration policy from Congress. The Immigration Act of 1990, which raised immigration levels to accommodate increasing worldwide demand to immigrate to the United States, was little more than an attempt to codify the realities that (unintentionally) resulted from the 1965 Act.

Prior to 1965 U.S. immigration law operated under guidelines set down in the 1924 Johnson-Reed Act. The Johnson-Reed Act placed strict numerical limits on the number of immigrants allowed to enter the United States and set national origins quotas, which were intended to maintain the existing ethnic make-up of the country. Every nation's immigration quota was established to reflect that national origin's percentage of the U.S. population at that time. Thus, the countries of northern and western Europe—the ancestral origins of most Americans at that time—received the lion's share of the available visas.

The 1965 Act sought to overturn the repugnant aspects of the national origin quota system and replace it with a system which placed all nations on an equal footing. Congress also sought to ensure that the number of immigrants entering the United States would not rise appreciably above the pre-1965 levels. A cap of 165,000 immigrants was placed on all non-western hemisphere countries and for the first time, at the insistence of Senator Sam Ervin, an annual numerical limitation of 120,000 was placed on immigration from the Western Hemisphere.

Elimination of the discriminatory national origins quotas and the establishment of what seemed to be a firm ceiling on immigration levels were among the factors that led me to co-sponsor this legislation. In my statement on the floor of the Senate, I said, "This measure will provide a much needed and long overdue change in immigration policy. It is a limited measure, since it does not make any substantial increase in the number of immigrants who can enter each year." However, unrecognized by virtually all of the bill's supporters, were provisions which would eventually lead to unprecedented growth in numbers and the transfer of policy control from the elected representatives of the American people to individuals wishing to bring relatives to this country.

Robert Kennedy, as attorney general and later a co-sponsor of the legislation in the Senate, testified before a House committee in 1964 and assessed what he believed would be the impact of the proposed changes in the immigration law. "I would say for the Asian–Pacific Triangle it (immigration) would be approximately 5000, Mr. Chairman, after which immigrants from that source would virtually disappear; 5000 immigrants would come in the first year, but we do not expect that there would be any great influx after that."

Secretary of State Dean Rusk assured Congress that, "Immigration now comes in limited volume," and that the proposed changes would not be "a drastic departure from the long-established immigration policy." Labor Secretary Willard Wirtz confidently predicted that the new law would result in a mere 23,000 workers being added to the labor force each year.

The reforms, as originally proposed by President Kennedy in 1963 and as drafted into legislation by its two prime sponsors, Senator Philip Hart and Congressman Emanuel Celler, were not intended to substantially increase overall numbers. They were intended to give immigration opportunities to people of all nationalities who were "especially advantageous" to the United States. Many conservatives in Congress, however, feared that these changes would lead to a deluge of Third World immigrants and eventually present a threat to the dominance of European culture in the United States.

To assuage their concerns, Michael A. Feighan, the chairman of the House Immigration Subcommittee, amended the proposed legislation to ensure that the top two immigration preference categories were set aside for people with family connections in the United States. It was not until one reached the third preference category that an immigrant's skills came into consideration. The thinking was that few Africans, Latins and Asiatics had the necessary family connections to qualify for these slots, thus ensuring the continuation of a predominantly European immigration flow.

What the sponsors of this amendment failed to recognize was that northern and western Europe after 20 years of postwar reconstruction was on the verge of an enormous economic boom. Those Europeans who might have liked to emigrate were prevented from doing so by the Iron Curtain. The third preference set aside for skilled workers was quickly filled by professional people from many of the Third World countries. Within a relatively short period of time they rather than the Europeans became the ones with relatives to fill up the first two preference categories.

The result of this miscalculation has been the creation of a situation in which the public domain is used for private gain. Virtually all immigration decisions today are made by private individuals who wish to bring relatives to live in this country. The government's role amounts to little more than rubber stamping the immigration decisions made by individual citizens and permanent residents. Immigration policy is now a vehicle by which people bring relatives to this country, rather than one by which the government decides who, among the millions of people who would like to come here, gets that chance.

For the ethnic interest groups that have benefitted politically from the current arrangement, U.S. immigration policy has become a virtual entitlement to be defended at all costs. In 1990, when Congress attempted to institute moderate revisions in the immigration law to make the selection process a little more merit based, the handful of groups that have dominated the immigrant flow since 1965 dug in their heels. In the end Congress proved powerless to reallocate existing visas and was forced to add additional immigration visas to provide opportunities for those without relatives in the United States.

While interests and ethnic groups whose constituents were shut out of the immigration process sought to gain something from reforming the immigration law in 1990, there were others who benefitted from the existing policy and sought to protect or expand the provisions that worked in their favor. The Hispanic-American and Asian-American lobbies made it clear that any gains that these other groups might make would not come at the expense of the provisions that benefitted immigrants from Latin America or Asia. The high levels of immigration from those countries during the 1970s and 1980s had in fact created huge backlogs of relatives waiting their turn to immigrate.

In the end Congress raised legal immigration quotas by about 40 percent to 700,000 a year. Combined with illegal immigration and unprecedented levels of refugee and political asylum admissions, the result of the 1990 law will mean the highest levels of immigration in U.S. history.

The law contained something for everyone who wanted more immigrants. Family-based immigration, which had skewed immigration preferences to the advantages of a handful of countries, was expanded to 465,000 annually. Additionally, illegal immigrants (primarily from those same countries) who received amnesty under IRCA, were granted 165,000 visas over a three-year period for relatives who did not qualify for the first amnesty. (These immigrants, many of whom are unskilled or low-skilled workers, will also satisfy the interests of industries that require these types of workers). One hundred forty thousand visas annually for immigrants with needed skills were added.

The Immigration Act of 1990 also offers 40,000 diversity visas which are to be allocated to citizens of countries that are considered to have been adversely affected by the 1965 law. These are primarily European countries that until 1965 had been the primary sources of immigration to the United States.

Business interests have added continuous force to the influx of immigrants. Throughout the 1960s and 1970s, American business got used to a constant abundance of labor which gave them the upper hand in setting wages and working conditions. (It is no accident that real wages have declined since the early 1970s.) As America's enormous baby boomer generation entered the labor force between 1965 and 1985, the laws of supply and demand were very much in the favor of business. Economist Charles R. Morris observes that, "New workers swelled the American labor force by about 50 percent in the past twenty years, shifting the average age and experience of workers sharply downward. Not surprisingly, with lots of cheap new workers mobbing the doorway, businessmen increased hiring instead of investing in labor-saving machinery. . . . Real wages and productivity were stagnant, and the business success stories were companies like McDonald's that learned how to "pan for gold in the low wage pool."

The Cuban and Vietnam Factors

Because of economic and political turmoil in Cuba in the fall of 1965, Fidel Castro suddenly announced that any Cuban (except men of military age) who wished to leave might do so. On October 3, President Johnson responded by announcing that any of those Cubans who so desired could come to the United States. By November of 1965, the United States and Cuban governments, with the Swiss acting as intermediary, had agreed that an "air bridge" would be established by which two charter flights a day would be permitted to land in Cuba and carry refugees back to the United States. From that time until those freedom flights were unilaterally stopped by

Cuba in 1973, some 270,000 Cuban refugees were admitted to the United States under this arrangement, many of them relatives of Cubans who had come earlier. The Cuban refugees of this period have been described as upper socio-economic class persons who were able, educated and successful. Many of them were professional and many already knew English well. The legal authority used to admit these airlift refugees was the parole authority of the attorney general of the United States. In 1966 Congress passed the Cuban Refugee Adjustment Act to enable them to become permanent resident aliens without first leaving the country to apply for the appropriate visa. From the beginning of the Castro regime in 1959 to the end of the airlift in 1973 some 677,158 Cuban refugees entered the United States.

The Cuban air bridge had barely ceased when events in Southeast Asia set in motion the largest mass immigration of refugees to the United States. Many of the first refugees from Vietnam were persons who had been closely associated with the United States in the war effort, in fact over 20,000 had been brought out to Guam even before the fall of Saigon on April 25, 1975. Between April and December of 1975, a total of 130,000 Indochinese refugees were admitted under parole provisions, many of them either relatives of U.S. citizens or closely allied with the war effort.

These initial refugees were quickly outnumbered by others throughout Indochina who sought admission after having escaped from South Vietnam, Cambodia or Laos. Then came the first of the boat people who had been expelled or who had escaped from Vietnam. Events in Southeast Asia forced the United States to respond. Massive numbers of refugees fled or were forced out, perhaps 1.2 million persons between 1975 and 1979. Tales of horror emerged of what these refugees endured; if their greatly overcrowded, marginally seaworthy craft survived, they were subjected to attack and plunder by pirates; and, on numerous occasions when they finally reached land in Thailand, Malaysia, Indonesia or Hong Kong, their boats with the desperate, starving survivors still aboard, were pushed back out to sea by countries that feared that if they let them land, they would not be able to get rid of them. Against this background, President Carter again made use of the parole authority and authorized the admission of 210,000 such refugees between July 1979 and September 1980.

Again in 1980 Castro allowed a mass exodus from Cuba, but this time the character of the refugees was different from that of the air bridge refugees of the early 1970s. Many Cubans on the boats from the port of Mariel in 1980 came from a variety of state-run institutions, including prisons. The Mariel boat lift eventually brought some 130,000 Cubans out, about 1.5 percent of the entire population of Cuba at the time.

CHAPTER V

Illegal Immigration

AT THE SAME TIME AS THE NUMBER OF LEGAL IMMIGRANTS HAVE BEEN increasing so has the number of those entering the United States illegally. The number of persons coming into the United States illegally increased greatly in the years following the end of WWII. In 1950 the United States had 416 ports of entry by land, sea and air. The border patrol force remained at about 1,100 persons while the apprehension of deportable aliens tripled, from 100,000 in 1946 to 300,000 in 1949. This period marked the beginning of the loss of control over illegal border crossings.

The number of deportable aliens rose rapidly in the 1960s and 1970s. In 1972 a half-million deportable aliens were apprehended. By 1977 the number had doubled. The Immigration Service estimated that in 1974 millions of undocumented aliens were living in the United States. In that year 274 million persons were checked at ports of entry and one million deportable aliens were apprehended.

The Immigration and Naturalization Service now estimates that approximately three million people enter this country illegally each year and about a quarter million—the equivalent of a medium-size city—settle permanently. We manage to deport only about 22,000 each year. It is estimated that with illegal immigration, refugees and asylees, total immigration is well in excess of one million people annually during the 1990s.

There is a growing body of evidence to suggest that we are paying a very heavy price for our failure to control our borders. A 1989 General Accounting Office (GAO) report found that 40 percent of the crack cocaine trade in this country is controlled by aliens. Two years earlier, the GAO reported that 50 percent of those arrested by the Los Angeles Police Department's drug task force were illegal aliens. In Santa Ana in neighboring Orange County fully 95 percent of the narcotics task force's arrests were of illegal aliens! In this respect it could be said that the United States is not only in the process of becoming a colony to the world but a colony to the underworld as well.

The price is also high in monetary terms. In a nation where 20 percent of our children live in poverty, in which 37 million people do not have access to basic health care services, an alarming share of our public assistance dollars are going to benefit illegal aliens. An April 1991 report from Los Angeles County's chief administrative officer, Richard B. Dixon, quantified the costs for just that one county. Dixon found that during the 1990–91 fiscal year the net cost to the county for providing health, education and welfare benefits to illegal aliens was $276.2 million. Half of the federal government's contribution to the AFDC program in Los Angeles County now goes to provide benefits to the children of illegal immigrants and Dixon warns the price tag for just that one program could reach $1 billion annually by the year 2000. Two-thirds of all babies born in public hospitals in Los Angeles at taxpayer expense are born to illegal alien mothers.

Similar strains on the public welfare are being seen in other parts of the country. According to Florida Senator Connie Mack, during 1989 illegal aliens were registering in Dade County public schools "at a rate of 755 per month; that's virtually two new teachers per day and one new school per month." In addition to the public financed tuition cost of $3,900 per pupil per year, there was an additional $136 million expense to provide temporary and permanent classroom space to accommodate the influx of illegal alien students.

By far the most powerful external force being exerted on our immigration policies comes from explosive population growth around the globe. Throughout the underdeveloped world, countries whose economies and ecologies cannot adequately accommodate the people they have now, populations are growing rapidly. The tension and conflict caused by crowding, rapid urbanization and economic despair have created unprecedented migratory pressures. Just to maintain the status quo, the struggling economies of the underdeveloped world will need to create more new jobs in the next decade than currently exist in the entire developed world.

The United States, with the most generous immigration policy of any nation, still absorbs a mere one percent of the annual worldwide population increase. The immigration policies of this country were not designed to cope with global population increases of one billion people every decade.

As recently as 1965 no one truly conceived the magnitude of the global population explosion. "In 1830, one billion people inhabited the Earth," writes Werner Fornos, president of the Population Institute. "A century passed before the population reached two billion. Thirty years later in 1960 it hit three billion; 15 years later four billion, and by 1986—only 11 years later—five billion . . . the six billion mark could be reached by 1995." Thus, since the 1965 immigration reforms (which were actually conceived in the 1950s), human population has doubled.

It was not until publication of Paul Ehrlich's landmark book, *The Population Bomb,* in 1970 that the issue of global population growth took hold on the national consciousness. Few analysts back then could project the significance of an exponential increase in world population. History had seen nothing like it. Its impact on international migration patterns is only now beginning to be understood. The United States must define and firmly enforce immigration policies that are in the national interest.

While it is difficult to estimate the power of the external forces that are driving ever-increasing numbers of people to migrate illegally, the United States itself must bear a large share of the blame. We have done little to stop or prevent illegal immigration, and in many ways have subtly encouraged it.

In 1986 when illegal immigration had reached unprecedented levels, Congress instituted employer sanctions, a law which prohibited the hiring of illegal aliens. Employer sanctions, a law first proposed by President Harry Truman, removed the lure of jobs that was drawing most illegal immigrants to this country. Merely putting such a law on the books with virtually no enforcement resulted in a 50 percent reduction in illegal immigration over the first three years. Yet, despite overwhelming evidence that enforcement of employer sanctions could significantly reduce illegal immigration, *that has not happened.* Lax enforcement of sanctions and rampant document fraud by illegal aliens seeking to circumvent the law allowed illegal immigration to skyrocket.

Similarly we have failed to do much to prevent illegal immigration at the border. While we know that 90 percent of illegal immigration takes place along 200 miles of border in California and Texas, there are fewer border patrol officers on duty along the United States-Mexico border at any given time than there are police officers patrolling the grounds of the U.S. capitol.

It is not merely that we do not take adequate steps to prevent or deter illegal immigration; in many respects we have instituted policies that encourage people to violate our immigration laws. In the United States we have bestowed nearly all the rights of citizenship on people who have settled in this country illegally, while requiring of them few of the duties of citizenship.

Congressional reapportionment for the 1990s, as was the case in the 1980s, will grant illegal aliens representation in Congress. As many as three of California's seven new seats in the House of Representatives will reflect the presence of large numbers of illegal immigrants in that state.

In many jurisdictions in this country, we have gone out of our way to ensure that social benefits are equally accessible to illegal aliens as they are to citizens. The California state legislature, even as it struggled to close a $14 billion fiscal 1992 budget deficit, voted to overturn a court decision which denied in-state tuition to illegal aliens at state-run universities. Thus, after a court had decided that the taxpayers of that state need not subsidize the higher education of people who are in the United States illegally, the California legislature actively took steps to ensure those benefits would continue to be handed out without regard to legal status. Governor Pete Wilson in the end vetoed the bill, but the legislative action itself is indicative of a changing attitude about the privileges and prerogatives of citizenship.

In New York City, a municipality perpetually on the brink of bankruptcy, former Mayor Ed Koch issued an executive order which prohibited city agencies from differentiating between citizens and illegal aliens when it came to disbursing public benefits. Similar policies exist in other cities.

Nationwide, the homeless population has grown into the millions. Yet when the city of Costa Mesa, California, sought to reserve federally subsidized housing for U.S. citizens and legal immigrants, U.S. Secretary of Housing and Urban Development Jack Kemp stepped in to assure illegal aliens equal access to public housing.

By our own actions, the United States is sending a message to the world that the right to live and receive benefits in this country is available equally to citizen and non-citizen alike. In a Senate debate on immigration policy in 1965, Senator Allen Ellender of Louisiana warned that, "There is a strange attitude in this country today on the part of some people who feel that this land and its material wealth do not rightfully belong to the citizens of this country, but, in effect, belong to the world's population at large."

The United States has also allowed its political asylum policies to be controlled by the people seeking asylum, rather than by our government. Political asylum was intended to protect those rare individuals who, due to unforeseen circumstances, could not safely return home or to aid persecuted individuals who escaped their oppressors while in U.S. jurisdiction. Before 1980 not more than 5000 people applied for political asylum each year; by 1990 the number of asylum seekers had exploded to more than 100,000 annually.

Virtually anyone from a country with a nondemocratic government (the vast majority of the human race) who manages to enter the United States can assure himself or herself of remaining here by simply asking for asylum. The system is so bogged down under the current volume of applicants that it can take years to adjudicate an asylum claim. Even if the claim is ultimately denied, the applicant has by that time been here long enough to establish claims for remaining in this country.

In two particular instances in the past several years, foreign governments have requested that the United States allow millions of their citizens to remain in this country as refugees or asylees because it served the interests of those governments. During the 1980s, close to 1.5 million Salvadorans and Nicaraguans fled the poverty and violence of their native countries and settled illegally in the United States. Even as the civil wars in those countries largely abated and democratically elected governments were installed, the governments of El Salvador and Nicaragua formally asked that the United States not return those citizens. In both cases foreign governments successfully asserted control over U.S. refugee and asylum policies. In acceding to these unprecedented requests, the United States in effect told the rest of the world that their excess population was a hardship that could be alleviated through massive resettlement in the United States.

In a world of growing populations and rising tensions, hardly a shot can be fired in anger without it having an impact on U.S. refugee or asylum policy. Modern communications have brought the horrors of the world in living color right into our living rooms.

Modern transportation has brought the victims and the potential victims to our shores. International events and modern technology, not the U.S. government, control refugee and asylum policy.

Because of the magnitude of violence in today's world, drawing arbitrary distinctions between victims is an unfortunate but necessary exercise. To someone whose life is in jeopardy these may seem like distinctions without differences. But to the United States and other countries that can grant sanctuary to only a small percentage of the world's oppressed, they are important distinctions. An Iraqi Kurd, for example, is someone who would probably meet the seemingly technical requirement of a "well-founded fear of persecution," based on membership in a particular ethnic group. Saddam Hussein has unquestionably singled out Kurds for slaughter. A Salvadoran, however, is merely (and certainly regrettably) someone who lives in a dangerous country where just about anybody can wind up on the wrong end of a bullet. A Haitian who comes to this country seeking political asylum is more often than not simply someone who comes from a very poor and overcrowded country—no better or worse off than anyone else unfortunate enough to have been born in Haiti.

Even those refugee decisions which are not directly influenced by the actions of foreign governments are rarely made simply out of humanitarian concerns. Decisions about who will receive refugee or political asylum status in the United States are very often dictated by the media, political pressure groups, and the ability of individuals to reach this country. It is very difficult for the government to deport a Salvadoran peasant whose prime motivation for coming here was to escape poverty. The fact that he is here—having much easier access to this country than an Iraqi Kurd—and the fact that he is part of a group large enough to constitute a community in the United States means that he is likely to be allowed to remain. (The United States cannot round up a million Salvadorans and ship them back.) We pass laws, as we did in 1990, that grant official recognition to policies we are powerless to control.

Domestic political interest groups have attempted to co-opt refugee policy to promote domestic policy objectives. The powerful anti-abortion movement has lobbied to make Chinese couples who wish to have more than one child eligible for refugee status in the United States. In 1990 Senator William Armstrong of Colorado introduced legislation that would have made hundreds of millions of Chinese eligible for refugee status as a means of expressing disapproval for their family planning policies.

Decisions about refugee status and political asylum in the United States are shaped by a variety of sources: foreign governments (both friendly and unfriendly), the media, political pressure groups and the people who claim to be refugees. Considerations have gone well beyond the simple desire of the American people to assist those who are truly persecuted.

The decade of the 1980s—if one includes legal immigration, illegal immigration, refugees and asylees—was the single greatest 10-year period of in-migration in the nation's history. It was almost entirely generated by exploding Third World populations, deteriorating economic conditions and political disorders in those countries.

Yet, notwithstanding these facts, Congress in 1990 responded to external and internal demands and increased legal immigration quotas to 700,000 per year.

Conclusions

Meanwhile the debate on immigration policies continues in Congress, among academics, editors and within the general public. The points at issue are cultural, political, economic and humanitarian. The contrasting views on the economic consequences of immigration have recently been presented by two authors. Julian Simon, Professor of Business Administration at the University of Maryland, advocates increasing the number of immigrant admissions by one million a year. He argues that such an increase will be good for the American economy and society.

George Borjas, University of California, Santa Barbara, disagrees. He asserts that recent immigrants are much less skilled than those of previous years. Immigrants in the 1950s averaged 0.4 school years more than native Americans. In the 1970s, he says immigrants had 0.7 fewer school years than natives. Today's immigrants are more likely to be unemployed, on welfare, or living in poverty than earlier immigrants (or natives). Borjas further says that immigrants of the late 1960s have a five percent higher poverty rate than natives in the time following their arrival, and that immigrants of the late 1970s had an 18 percent higher poverty rate. Nine percent of immigrant households are on welfare overall, but 26 percent of households headed by an immigrant from the Dominican Republic are listed as poor by government standards; the same is true of 13 percent of households headed by a Mexican, 17 percent of those headed by a

Cuban, and ten percent of those headed by a Filipino. Eight percent of native households are classified as poor.

Borjas predicts that the typical immigrant who arrived in the 1970s is not likely to reach income parity with natives during his lifetime. This difference he attributes to the emphasis given in the current immigration laws to family unification.

The Borjas conclusions are supported by Dan Stein of the Federation for American Immigration Reform (FAIR). He disputes the claim of some that immigrants pay more in taxes than they use in benefits, suggesting that those who make this claim use a definition of benefits that excludes medical care, education, public housing and a wide range of other social services, and that they limit their comparisons only to the cost of Federal benefits, ignoring most state and local programs from which the immigrants benefit.

Dan Stein also challenges the claim that we need immigrants today to replace the baby boomer generation as they reach retirement age, pointing out that the average age of today's immigrants is almost identical to that of the native population and that the typical immigrant today will retire and begin collecting Social Security benefits at about the same time that those baby boomers reach retirement age. He also challenges assertions, some of which he calls myths (others half-truths), and statistical representations or misrepresentations, that we are an aging society in need of new workers, that immigrants have higher incomes than natives, and that immigrants create more jobs than they take over. This, he says, may be true of the total number of jobs, but not of quality jobs.

The labor shortage claim is of course a tried-and-true tactic for manipulating immigration policy to benefit powerful business interests. The same arguments were used by business to increase immigration in the mid-1960s—when the baby boom generation was just beginning to enter the work force! In 1964 *Business Week* magazine fretted about a shortage of older workers: "Immigrants are also expected to help fill the dwindling ranks of native workers in the prime age group—35 to 44 years old. Without immigrants . . . this group would decline in the 1960s by about 70,000, reflecting the slowdown in births during the 1930s."

In fact, the supply of labor has almost nothing to do with the general health of a nation's economy. Japan and Germany, two countries with very low birth rates, have more than adequately compensated for labor shortages through capital investment in efficient methods of production. We, on the other hand, have continually given in to the demands of our least efficient industries and imported immigrants to do the work of machines. We have paid the price in declining competitiveness, declining educational standards and a growing underclass.

The United States cannot regain its competitive standing in the world by importing low wage workers from other countries. On the one hand, it engenders conditions this country cannot and should not tolerate. In New York's Chinatown today, we have allowed a sweatshop garment industry to flourish on virtual slave labor. Thousands of illegal Chinese immigrants toil under conditions that would have shocked Jacob Riis, with their meager wages going to pay the exorbitant demands of the organized crime syndicates that smuggled them into this country. On the other hand, in the modern age a nation's wealth and prosperity is secured by high worker productivity and capital investment, not by the availability of low-wage labor.

Moreover, in the emerging global marketplace, our immigration objectives with regard to competitiveness are becoming increasingly confusing. Multinational corporations do not retain the national identities or loyalties, and will set up operations wherever it is most advantageous. Under these circumstances, it makes little sense to transfer workers when corporations are just as likely to establish production facilities in immigrants' home countries.

That we have the capacity to absorb more workers and more people, Stein acknowledges, may be true, but the matter at issue is not number but conditions under which immigrants are received and absorbed into the economy and the larger society. He also challenges the myth that immigrants have always succeeded and notes that successes in the past occurred under very different social and economic conditions, those marked by exploitation along the way.

Stein's positions are at odds with some of the judgments, prophecies and projections made by Ben Wattenberg in his new book, *The First Universal Nation,* published by Macmillan. According to Wattenberg, a fellow at the American Enterprise Institute, the new immigration bill, which increases immigration by 40 percent, "means a big boost for existing businesses because it expands the customer base" and "coupled with recent unexpected increases in fertility . . . means America will grow twice as fast as expected— 45 million more people in the next few decades."

There are four major areas in which effective action is possible and necessary if the United States is to deal with immigration problems. First, the flow of illegal immigration should be stopped. To accomplish this objective, the number of border patrol personnel should be increased. Even though 90 percent of all illegal alien apprehensions occur along a 90-mile section of border between the United States and Mexico, present personnel are inadequate to control even that small part of land borders of the United States which extend for more than 6000 miles. There is a need in our structure of defense, especially that against illegal immigration and illegal transport of drugs and other contraband into the United States, for a new institutional force, possibly as an extension or complement to the Coast Guard. The contemplated reduction of the number of persons in the armed forces would supply a personnel source. With fewer than 17,000 employees and a budget of about $750 million, the Immigration and Naturalization Service is expected to perform work of such volume and variety as that performed in fiscal year 1986 when the INS processed 60,000 refugees, adjudicated 600,000 legal immigrants, processed 45,000 asylum applications, naturalized 280,000 aliens and admitted over 10 million non-immigrants—tourists, students and business persons. And, in addition, INS and border patrol agents undertook enforcement functions along the borders of the United States with Canada and Mexico. Subsequently, enforcement of employer sanctions law required the same officers in 1987 to inspect 320 million persons, both citizens and aliens entering the United States over land boundaries, to deport 22,000 aliens, prosecute over 23,000 violations of immigration and nationality laws, visit 800,000 employers to inform them of the new sanctions law, and apprehend and return to their home countries nearly a million illegal aliens. In addition, the border patrol performs non-immigration functions, including interdiction of smuggled weapons, alcoholic beverages, parrots, animal skins, narcotics and other contraband.

Second, as a part of the enforcement programs, employer sanctions should be vigorously pursued. A General Accounting Office study made in 1985 found that employer sanctions had been effective in a number of countries where enforcement had been thorough and fines had been stiff.

Third, actions should be taken to encourage countries from which the illegal immigrants come to stop or discourage emigration, and the countries should be helped to establish viable economies which will relieve the pressure on their people to attempt the illegal entry into the United States. Action to improve economic conditions and to provide job opportunities, though it came late, has been an effective force for stabilizing the movement of Puerto Ricans into the

United States. Comparable efforts might well be effective in relationships with Mexico and other Central and South American countries.

Fourth, laws bearing on legal immigration should be changed to give the United States more control over both numbers and quality of immigrants. In fiscal year 1989, legal immigration totaled about 600,000, not including 490,000 illegal aliens who were granted amnesty. Of these 600,000, some 435,000 were relatives of people living in the United States as citizens or as resident aliens. Of the kinship admissions, about 218,000 were immediate relatives (spouses, minor children or parents of adult citizens) who can enter without any numerical limitations, and 84,000 had been admitted as refugees. According to an article in *The Washington Post* of October 7, 1990, by Barry Chiswick, chairman of the Department of Economics at the University of Illinois, Chicago, two preference categories in the law are reserved for professional and skilled workers and allow for the admission of 54,000 persons. But Chiswick notes nearly 60 percent of this category of visas were used by the spouses and dependent children of applicants. Fewer than 22,600 immigrants by his estimate, or less than four percent of non-amnesty immigrants admitted in 1989 were skill tested. Certainly the unrestricted immigration of the immediate relatives of United States citizens (spouses, aged parents, minor children) should continue. The other preference admissions, adult married children of United States citizens (over 13,000 in 1989), spouses and unmarried children of resident aliens (nearly 113,000 admitted in 1989), married children of United States citizens and their families (nearly 27,000) and siblings of United States citizens and their families (over 64,000) should be reexamined. Immigrants entering under the kinship category or as refugees are not currently screened for skill levels, professional status or likely economic success. It is clear that the kinship standard is too freely applied, making admission to the United States rest on biological and generative conditions, rather than other standards which, if applied, would be fairer to those asking admission to the United States and which might improve the quality of immigrants admitted to the United States.

As to admission of refugees, first the United States should be more careful about generating refugees through irresponsible intervention in the affairs of other countries, when that intervention is almost certain to create political refugees. We should screen refugee applicants to be more certain that they are truly refugees, and should require other countries to carry a larger refugee burden than they now carry.

And finally, the federal government should assume more responsibility for the cultural and economic integration of immigrants into American life.

It is not the purpose of this chapter to settle the controversy between the advocates and challengers of present immigration, legal and illegal; between those who advocate more restrictive laws or more liberal laws, whatever the reason given: humanitarian relief of poverty in other parts of the world; providing a haven for political refugees, whether created by our military and political involvements or by those of other nations, or by internal political conflicts; for economic reasons, such as improving our own work force by introducing more workers, younger workers or more skilled workers. Rather, its purpose is to raise and examine the question of whether we have adequate control over our borders to control passage of persons, and passage or transport of materials, especially money and drugs, or the combination "drug-money." It is also the purpose of this chapter to look at conditions causing or encouraging illegal immigration, and to examine legal immigration to determine the extent to which that immigration, both as to numbers and quality of immigrants, is properly within our control. Finally, its purpose is to consider what measures can be or should be taken to establish or reestablish our control in a rational, historically defensible manner over passage of persons and of materials into the United States.

CHAPTER VI

Economic and Financial

CLASSICAL ECONOMIC COLONIALISM HAS THREE DISTINCTIVE MARKS.
First, major investments in the colony are made by the mother country, or by citizens, or financial institutions of that country; second, the colony exports raw materials to the other country and imports manufacturers' products; third, the financial institutions of the colony are dominated by institutions in the mother country, and the currency of the colony is either that of the mother country or is closely tied to that currency. At the height of British imperial power the Royal Navy ruled the seas, and the British pound ruled the land. The neo-colonial status of the United States is marked by the same features that defined classical colonialism. The first is increased investment from outside, not by or from an imperial mother country, but increasingly by foreign countries or individuals or institutions from such countries operating in the relatively open United States investment field. The principal instrument for such investment and accompanying control is the multinational corporations which have nearly all of the attributes of a sovereign nation.

The United States does attempt to restrict some forms of direct foreign investment in minerals, communications, air transport, nuclear energy, and inland shipping, although foreigners are generally permitted to purchase non-controlling interest in voting stock even in companies operating in these restricted fields. The growth of the multinational corporations had made it increasingly difficult to control fiscal and commercial activities. For example, the United States government's efforts to prevent the export of U.S. technology can be frustrated when the export is protected or covered by the immunity of a multinational corporation. The significance and danger of such control over economic interests of the United States was made clear by the president of a major oil company during the oil embargo of 1973. He reported that his company had in fact allocated a larger share of the company's foreign oil production to the United States during the embargo than was warranted on the basis of other countries' shares of company business before the embargo. He then questioned whether as the president of a multinational company he was justified in favoring the United States.

In a comparable situation, Dressen Industries used the cover of multinationalism to justify the sale of oil pipeline technology to the Russians, despite protests from the Reagan Administration. In August of 1980 a subcommittee of the Committee on Interstate and Foreign Commerce of the House of Representatives held hearings on foreign investment in the United States and on the economic control and other consequences of such investments. Direct investment in the United States business and financial institutions, the committee noted, tripled between 1970 and 1978 from $13 billion to approximately $49 billion. On a percentage basis, foreign investment in those years had increased by 99 percent in contrast with an increase of U.S. investments abroad by only 66 percent. In the years since 1980, foreign investments have continued to grow. In 1989 the United States Commerce Department estimated that foreign investments exceeded $1.5 trillion.

We should be concerned not only about the volume of foreign investments but the particular industries, real property, and service companies in which the investments are being placed. Americans have come to accept that the Japanese are investors in Toyota, the Germans in Volkswagen, the Dutch in Shell Oil and the British in British Petroleum. Foreign investments have been extended into many other fields, including products which are in daily use in the United States, including such things as Alka-Seltzer, Clorox, Borax, Lipton tea, Pepsodent toothpaste, Kool cigarettes, Beechnut baby food, Libby fruits and vegetables, J & B Scotch, Good Humor and Baskin-Robbins ice cream, Capitol records, Timex watches, Hills Bros. coffee and SOS soap pads.

Foreigners have acquired a controlling interest in such well-known corporations as Standard Oil of Ohio, American Motors, Howard

Johnson's, International House of Pancakes, Stouffer Hotels, A & P and Grand Union supermarkets, Gimbels and Saks Fifth Avenue. The list grows nearly every day.

In 1985 a *New York Times* article described the extent of foreign-owned companies:

> An American family, without realizing it, could live in an apartment building owned by foreign insurance companies, buy its groceries from a German-owned chain (A & P) or a French-owned one (Grand Union) and purchase its clothes from a British-owned department store chain (Saks Fifth Avenue, Gimbels or Marshall Field & Co.) using cash from its Hong Kong-owned bank (Marine Midland). The husband or wife might work in a skyscraper owned by Britain's Duke of Westminster (Wells Fargo Tower in Los Angeles), and the family might decide to vacation at a Kuwaiti-owned resort (Kiowa Island, South Carolina).
>
> The family might then drive to its vacation in a car made by American Motors (46 percent French-owned), get aggravated by a Mack Truck (41 percent French-owned) roaring past and then soothed by hearing "Sentimental Journey" (the ex-Beatle Paul McCartney owns the copyright) on the radio.

Foreign investment has been extended into the publishing of newspapers, magazines, books, including school textbooks, and most recently into television and motion picture production. Sony Corporation took over Columbia Pictures in 1989. Then in 1990 Matsushita acquired MCA, Inc., which owns Universal Studios, MCA Records and G.P. Putnam's Sons publishing house. Sony, when it acquired Paramount, gave assurance that the company would not influence movie scripts and topics. Matsushita would not give comparable assurances. While foreign ownership of television stations is forbidden in the United States, there is no ban on ownership of production companies. Professor Ishikawa, of Seijo University, expressed concern that the electric company's ownership of the studio could usher in "an age of cultural censorship." MGM-Pathe is owned by an Italian businessman (or was as this was written), and Rupert Murdoch, an Australian, has bought 20th Century Fox.

Reports, news stories and headlines continue to emphasize our continuing loss of control over our economy. *The New York Times* of January 28, 1990, noted the growing stake of Canadians in the American economy with about $62 billion of direct investment, which ranks Canada fourth behind the British, Japanese and Dutch in such investments. *Portfolio Magazine* of June 1989 reports that in

1970 the Netherlands held 16 percent of the foreign investments in the United States while the Japanese held two percent, and that by 1986 the Japanese share had grown to 11 percent while the Dutch held over 20 percent.

The second economic indicator of colonial dependence, export of raw materials and importation of manufactured or processed products, is more and more evident in U.S. trade with other nations. One of the causes of the American Revolutionary War was British insistence on this relationship of dependency. Today we ship or sell timber to Japan and import fiberboard. We ship scrap metal to Japan and import automobiles; we ship coal to Germany and import chemical and synthetic products. Foreign countries, or their nationals, persons and companies, are not only importing raw materials from the United States, but buying land and mines and forests that produce the materials. Japan, for example, has bought thousands of acres of farmland in the United States. Food exports to Japan are largely a part of a continuous Japanese-owned process with Japanese companies owning the land on which the products are grown, the business that purchases and processes the harvests, and the companies that ship the materials to Japan. The Japanese are also heavy investors in coal production, forests, fisheries and most recently in beef production. Companies from other countries also have large and growing holdings in the United States resources. The French government controls coal mines in Virginia and Kentucky through its state-owned enterprise Charbonnages de France. West Germany has comparable coal holdings in the Appalachian area, while British Petroleum owns coal mines in Illinois and in Indiana.

The third characteristic of economic colonial status is the absence of control over the domestic monetary system. Loss of control in this area is more serious as a threat to the economic and financial system of the country than is increased ownerships in land, minerals and in real property, factories, machines, equipment, etc. Financial power is more fluid. It is more easily manipulated and transferred, redirected, even withdrawn. Formal acknowledgment of this fiscal dependency occurred during the Nixon Administration when the dollar was not only devalued, but allowed to float, subject to the pressures of international money markets.

The federal budget has shown a deficit of significant amounts for more than 15 years, rising from $73.7 billion in 1976 to $212.2 billion in 1986; declining to about $150 billion a year in 1987, '88 and '89; and then rising to over $220 billion in 1990, followed by predictions of a $282 billion deficit in 1991, and a $348 billion deficit in 1992. Federal debt has risen from $709 billion in 1980 to two trillion, 400 billion dollars in 1990.

In 1983 foreign interests held treasury bonds worth approximately $164 billion. As the national debt has continued to rise, there has been an accompanying rise in foreign treasury bond ownership. In 1985 the treasury had become so dependent on foreign purchasers that a special bond was offered, guaranteeing anonymity for the purchaser even from the U.S. governments, thus indicating a willingness to take money from unfriendly government drug dealers and friendly dictators. Recently a Wall Street analyst at a financial conference startled participants, or seemed to startle them, by stating that the U.S. economy was being helped by an injection of drug money from various sources approaching $200 billion annually.

The recent and continuing BCCI bank scandal demonstrates the inadequacy of supervision or knowledge of foreign investments, both source of investment funds and placement. A 1985 publication by the International Trade Administration of the United States Government, an agency in the Department of Commerce, noted "the data in this report are not strictly comparable to the other major statistical series on foreign direct investment in the U.S." and admitted or acknowledged that a "major portion" of its contents was taken from newspaper and magazine articles.

Off-shore banks and financial institutions offer foreign investors access to U.S. financial markets and ways of buying into U.S. corporations, buying real estate and mines, and making other kinds of investment without being identified. Persons and institutions in the Netherlands Antilles, a group of islands in the West Indies with a population of 250,000, are reported to own almost 800,000 acres of United States farm, forest and grazing land, ranking with the United Kingdom, Canada, West Germany and Hong Kong as one of the top five investors in U.S. agricultural lands. The Cayman Islands in the West Indies, a dependency of Jamaica, having a population of about 18,000 persons, had in 1985 over 18,000 registered corporations and 450 banks.

Meanwhile, the balance of payments continues to run against the United States. The first quarter of 1991 showed an account surplus of $10.2 billion, the first surplus since 1982. This surplus was largely due to cash contributions from countries such as Japan and Saudi Arabia with major payments on their Desert Storm accounts. Between 1982 and 1991, the balance on current accounts ranged from a minus $5 billion 868 million in 1982 to a deficit of over $160 billion in 1987, following which the negative balance has declined slowly to $92 billion in 1990.

Today the dollar is over-extended and unstable. The dollar continues to be the key international currency. Countries use the dollar to settle accounts, to price commodities and store liquid assets, but its strength is almost as much political as it is economic. German marks and Japanese yen have been gaining strength against the dollar for 25 years. The Europeans are testing their own currency. The ECU has plans to shift to it in the future. There are good reasons to believe that the dollar will lose its position of superiority and become a competing currency in the near future unless the United States takes action to strenghen its economic position and sustain its currency.

A year ago there was danger that the Middle East oil producing countries, operating in the OPEC association, might leave the dollar zone. The Gulf War has postponed that possibility, but the United States' dependency on foreign oil, much of it from the Middle East, continues unabated, and the nation is without any comprehensive energy policy or program.

The trade imbalance between the United States and Germany and Japan was hailed by *The Wall Street Journal* as far back as 1986 as the top economic peril to the United States, surpassing the national debt as a threat to the dollar and to economic stability of the world economy. An indication of the dependency of the dollar on economic and fiscal powers outside the United States showed clearly in 1986 and 1987 when the dollar came under heavy selling pressure and Japan was called upon, or moved, to intervene by making large dollar purchases, while at the same time using moral persuasion and implied, if not formal, capital controls to discourage Japanese banks and other Japanese holders of dollars from dumping their dollar holdings. In September of 1989 the services and investment sectors of the United States showed, according to the U.S. Commerce Department, a deficit (principally because of increased earnings by foreigners on assets held in the United States) for the first time in 30 years.

The reasons for our neo-colonial economic status are multiple. First, there is lack of clear policy on the part of the United States government. "Free trade" is a covering slogan obstructing or delaying positive intervention. It is espoused principally by multinational businesses and financial institutions. While other nations impose serious limitation on imports from the United States, especially of agricultural products, the Japanese at one point excluded aluminum baseball bats made in America on the grounds that the bats were produced under inadequate control standards. Some countries use the old defense that they are protecting infant industries, a questionable defense since aged or middle-aged industries may well have as good a claim to defense, depending on the nature of attack upon them.

Supporters of the United States policy of neutrality or openness to foreign investment, with accompanying loss of control, claim many benefits from such intervention: jobs are created from infusion of foreign funds into the United States, especially into depressed areas; our balance of payments position is improved by the in-flow of foreign investments; federal debt financing is aided. One secretary of commerce, Malcolm Baldridge, made the arguments that foreign money coming into the United States helped keep interest rates down, and Fred Bergsten, assistant treasury secretary for Internal Affairs in the Carter Administration, saw an advantage in getting "other nations hooked on our economy." Evidently, Bergsten was taking a leaf from the British policy of getting colonies and others "hooked" on the pound and then devaluing it as the simplest way of taxing the subject people.

The U.S. Chamber of Commerce, reflecting their views of international bankers and multinational corporations, in defense of foreign intrusions into the U.S. financial and industrial world, in the mid-1980s did accept this same optimistic view in saying that "like any investment, no matter what the source, foreign investment does bring about a wide range of benefits to the U.S. economy as a whole. Any capital injection has the effect of increasing the number of jobs, the opportunity to retrain local workers in more sophisticated skills, the creation of payrolls, increased tax revenues which can help revitalize a depressed area, and a whole series of ripple effects such as increased purchases of local supplies and raw materials, increased shipping and transportation revenues, increased subcontracting relating to facilities and services." The report does not acknowledge that the same results might be accomplished by U.S. investments, does not acknowledge that shipping costs, for the most part, go to foreign shipping interests, nor does the report explain why with all of these advantages unemployment runs high in the United States and the balance of payments continues to run against the United States.

Various studies by government and private institutions report: that the largest suppliers of funds used by foreign-owned firms in the United States are U.S. banks and other U.S. credit sources; that foreign investors are buying American companies with only 20 to 30 percent of their own capital, while borrowing 70 to 80 percent from American banks; that increased foreign direct investment is not primarily investment of foreign capital, but foreign-controlled investment of capital raised in the United States.

The Chamber of Commerce claims to increased job creation is not sustained by the general trend in unemployment or by a careful look at employment patterns related to foreign investment and control. New plant construction, or the establishment of new industries, is not the general route of foreign investors. On the contrary, the general practice of foreign investors is to purchase American companies or merge with them. A large percentage of the two to three million Americans employed by foreign firms would likely be employed in the same or comparable jobs under American management and ownership if the takeovers had not happened.

There is no overwhelming evidence that foreign owners and investors have introduced new and advanced technology into the United States, but they have acquired advanced U.S. technology, which may be used in U.S. production, but most certainly will be transferred to the home country. The move of the Japanese into the U.S. semiconductor and computer industries is illustrative. With Japanese government support, Japanese corporations bought their way into the U.S. electronics industry.

Advocates of free trade forget that one objective of the American Revolution was protection of U.S. industry, and that Jefferson appealed to the American people to go along with him in "buying American" even though it might be more expensive for them to do so, and John Adams warned that one cost of the revolution would be that of changing habits in dress, equipage, and in other ways, but that such costs were part of the price of freedom and happiness. Bob Hope and some other celebrities now appear in television spots urging Americans to buy American.

Foreign countries, principally Japan, argue that the United States should clean up its act and become more competitive, that we should save and invest more; that United States businesses should stop pursuing short-term profits, take a longer view, improve research and technology and apply it commercially, improve our educational program, etc. There is substance to each of these recommendations, but response to all or each of them would still leave the United States at a disadvantage.

Our basic disadvantage against the Japanese and other competitors arises from two comprehensive, almost structural conditions. One major factor bearing on our social and trade disadvantage has been the costs of building, maintaining and financing our defense establishment. Defense spending bears upon the economic conditions of the United States and on its trade position in two ways: one, in its effect on the general economy of the United States, and the other, in its bearing on the competitive position of countries like Germany and Japan who are serviced and protected by the U.S. military establishment, supported largely by the U.S. economy through its tax-paying persons and institutions.

U.S. military expenditures have been on the rise since the end of the Korean War, rising to approximately $90 billion a year in 1976 and $95 billion in 1977, then to $299 billion in 1990. The estimate for 1992 is $315 billion.

Although there is some disagreement among analysts and economists about the effect of military expenditures on the general economy, it is generally accepted that the effect, in contrast with the effect of nonmilitary expenditures of relative magnitude, is negative. A comprehensive study on the economics of military spending, prepared and published in the mid-1980s by the Center on Budget and Policy Priorities, is a kind of Bible for the advocates and defenders of military expenditures as an aid to economic stability and growth. The study was supported by grants from the Rockefeller Brothers Fund and other sources.

The report never quite gets to the heart of the matter. The paper concludes boldly that the economic impact of military spending is only marginally different from that of other forms of federal spending. This comparison is, of course, not the important one. Comparison of the effects and consequences of military expenditures relative to nonmilitary and nongovernment expenditures is the important one. The report acknowledges that if higher military expenditures are financed by deficits (as they have been since 1970), economic disorder, especially inflation, is likely to follow. The report cites value of technological spin-offs from military research, and cites job creation as an additional benefit. Those who are critical of defense expenditures, both as to its relative and absolute effect on the general economy, seem to have the better case. They, speaking principally through the Center for Defense Information in Washington, DC, assert that one-third of all U.S. research and development funds are spent for military purposes, that there is little civilian fallout from such research, that the United States is and has been losing its lead in commercial technology to other nations, and that for this reason and others is falling behind in world markets. They point out that in countries in which very small percentages of government money is spent on military research and development, notably Germany and Japan, that annual rates on manufacturing productivity have been two to three times higher than the rate of such growth in the United States.

More directly discernible and measurable as a force bearing on relative economic strength of the United States and other nations, especially Germany and Japan, is the amount of money the United States spends, and has been spending for the defense of those countries, and countries that were and may feel that they are threatened by them. If the estimate that approximately 50 percent of our defense budget is attributable to direct costs of preparations to defend and stabilize Germany and Japan and other countries that we are obligated to defend, principally Korea and Taiwan, comparison of trade balance advantage of Germany and Japan over the United States is roughly equal to that of 50 percent. Assuming that there is a rough equivalence between these two figures, it is reasonable and fair to conclude that in the years since their economic recovery after the war, Germany and Japan should have paid a larger share of common defense expenses, far beyond the limited contributions they have made to support troops stationed in the respective countries, and that it would have been in order to impose a defense duty on goods imported into the United States from those countries during those years. And, that such a duty is justified now to help pay for that part of the U.S. federal debt created by borrowings to pay defense costs in previous years.

If such duties had been in place over the last 20 years, we would not be witnessing the United States government acting through the secretary of state bargaining for payments from countries that are the immediate and long term beneficiaries of our intervention in the Gulf War. The United States would not be close to becoming in its economic world status the "pitiful, helpless giant" as once described by President Richard Nixon, or even a pitiable, almost helpless giant, not because of its lack of power, but because of its unwillingness to mobilize and use its economic power in balance with its military power.

The second major factor putting us at a disadvantage in world trade competition is more complex and includes consumption and work habits.

The advocates of the simpler and more direct kind of protection argue that the old standards for determining what is fair and what is unfair in international trade are not being applied. The opponents of that kind of simple protectionism say that the old standards are no longer applicable. They are right.

If international trade is to be fair, obviously there is a need to find other standards of judgment. Almost every day the press carries articles and editorials indicating what those standards should be. *The Wall Street Journal* also reported (December 17, 1986) that to the dismay of the United States (especially as it bears on the trade imbalance), Europeans (especially the West Germans) are resisting our urging that they spend more. The case of one German was given as an example of the resistance. When this German's Volkswagen Beetle failed to pass a federal automobile inspection, the owner said that he would not consider borrowing money to buy a car. "Better to walk than to borrow," he said. Washington, meanwhile, continues to urge West Germany and other European governments to give their citizens more pocket money through lower interest rates and tax cuts. They will then spend more on consumer goods, even to the point where they will go beyond buying nationally produced goods and begin to "buy American," as Bob Hope urges us to do. Germans, it seems, are not even "buying German." At the same time, Americans are being urged to buy new cars, even to buy German, and are in fact doing so—BMWs, Mercedeses, Audis, and to a lesser degree Volkswagens.

The Japanese, like the West Germans, are also uncooperative consumers. In their case, it is not so much automobiles as food. Jim Fallows, in a November 1986 article in *The Atlantic,* notes that most Japanese are thin. Fallows reports that the average American ingests 800 calories a day more than does the average Japanese—3,393 calories to 2,593. Allowing for some natural differences in size, this is still a significant difference and may explain why the average American is approximately twenty pounds overweight. Meanwhile, the Japanese market for American rice and soybeans is severely restricted.

Overeating and being overweight have been democratized in the case of the United States. We are the greatest popular overeaters and overconsumers in the history of the world with possibly two exceptions: the Ik, an African mountain tribe whose members, by report, gorge themselves on a good day's kill without thought for other people or for their own tomorrow; and the Romans, who overconsumed but did not put on weight by using the vomitorium as an adjunct to the dining room. Sales of over-the-counter emetics are increasing in the United States.

Today, "We the People," as noted by Ronald Reagan in his State of the Union message, make up five percent of the world's population, yet we consume 25 percent of the world's production of fossil fuel. Overall annual consumption of material resources by the United States is more than twice that of Western Europe, four times that of Eastern Europe, and cannot even be compared realistically to consumption in other countries and areas of the world.

We have five percent of the world's population and we have 50 percent of its automobiles—one car for every 1.8 persons. Approximately 15 to 20 percent of our material production is used to pay for the construction and maintenance of these automobiles and 15 percent of the world's annual production of petroleum is used each year to fuel them. In an eight-hour day, the average American works approximately one and one-half hours to support his automobile. It has been suggested that any person who steals an automobile in the United States should be punished by having to support it.

Yet, the world evidently is not satisfied with our performance. We are being asked to consume more: Arab oil producers want us to use more oil in order to stabilize the Middle East. Japanese, Korean, and German automobile producers urge more of their cars upon us, even using American parts as a sales aid. Argentines and Australians ask us to consume more beef and mutton. Brazilians and Colombians urge more coffee consumption on us; South American, Central American, Caribbean, and Pacific sugar producers would have us use more sugar; Asian, Middle Eastern, and South American producers of drugs continue to supply the American market.

Obviously, these and similar nations will just have to consume, or overconsume, their share of the world's production and throw away the excess. However, if they are unable to do so, their excess should be excluded from the U.S. market, especially if it involves grave threats to the personal health and safety of American citizens. For example, our duty on imports should reflect the differential between the percent of gross national product spent on defense of the United States and that spent by other countries or organizations, especially those that we are obligated by treaty and agreement to defend—notably, NATO, Japan, Taiwan, South Korea. If we are to be overdefended, so should they. They should bear their share of the overdefense.

If our highways are overcrowded and dangerous, theirs should be as crowded and dangerous; if there is insufficient space for highways, as in Japan, they should still be required to continue buying cars until their car-to-person ratio is comparable to ours. Falling short of that, they should pay a duty on any of their cars exported to the United States. They could produce a car that runs in place—since, by report, the Japanese run in place because there is too little room for jogging.

Similar standards should be applied in other areas. Citizens of countries exporting manufactured goods to the United States should be required to be overweight in roughly the same proportion as Americans, providing a market for American agricultural products. If not, they should pay a penalty for their own or their government's self-discipline.

Obviously, countries that export goods to the United States and still have the six-day work week (Japan and West Germany) should be penalized on two counts: (1) the excessive production of goods on the sixth day; (2) the underconsumption of goods because they have only one free day a week for leisure activities and leisure consumption.

Bearing on our competitive position in the world economy and our state of colonial dependency is the general condition of the U.S. economy, but especially the national debt. That debt is now over three trillion dollars and it is predicted that, if present trends and policies continue, the debt will rise above four trillion dollars, three-fourths of which will be held by individuals of great wealth, foreigners and Americans, by financial institutions and by corporations. The other one-fourth will be held by agencies of the federal government and by state and local governments and their agencies. The annual cost of servicing the three-fourths are held by the federal government and its agencies will come close to $300 billion a year. The federal government will then be, as it is now in slightly lesser measure, the instrument through which taxes, levied largely on wages and salaries, will be collected, transferred and transformed into capital, on which or from which capital gains will be earned, or other forms of tax-privileged income. The federal government will thus be the agency for continuing concentration of wealth and power over wealth beyond U.S. control.

PART III

CHAPTER VII

Colonialism—The Fourth Factor

THE FOURTH MARK OF COLONIAL DEPENDENCY IS EITHER THE IMPOSITION of the mother country's culture on the colony, or dependent society, or the gradual acceptance of that culture by the dependent country. This cultural acceptance or imposition is most often manifest in two cultural areas, religion and language, with religious change in some cases preceding change in language. Among the European colonial nations the Spanish were most aggressive in pressing for conversion of the people of their colonies. Clergy accompanied the conquistadors, or followed closely behind them. Oppression, exploitation, atrocities of varied kind were excused, even justified, by assurances that the victims had received in place of what they had suffered and of what they had lost, the true faith, including a promise of eternal salvation and happiness. The French colonialists, in the American manifestation, did not tie religious conversion as closely to colonial activities as did the Spanish, rather leaving it to missionaries, especially Jesuits, to look to the conversion of the savage people. Names of missionaries, such as Hennepin and Marquette, mark the trails of the French explorers as Franciscan missions mark the Spanish movement through Mexico and California. Portuguese became the language of natives of Brazil, Spanish the language of Mexico and most of South America. Canadian Indians, many of them, took to the French language. The English colonial masters were more interested in commerce than they were in religion, leaving religion to the churchmen, although willing to benefit through sale of cotton cloth to natives who had been persuaded by the missionaries to wear clothes, even in warm weather.

The English colonists to America, most of whom came to escape religious persecution or oppression in England, did not have any strong commitment to convert the Indians, at least in the early years of colonial settlement. As years and decades passed, most of the major religions in the United States established missionary societies devoted to converting Indians and each other. The effort moved Sam Houston, in talking to Alexis de Tocqueville during de Tocqueville's visit to the United States in 1831, to observe that there were two things that should not be given to Indians: the first was brandy and the second was Christianity. No serious or effective move was made by the English to convert the natives in Australia, although much work was done among the Europeans, principally the English and Irish, who had been sent to the colony as punishment for various crimes, or who had gone on their own seeking fortune or change. Few of those who came to Australia, at least before the beginning of the 20th century, had come for higher purposes.

The mark of English colonialism was usually domination of trade and the imposition or establishment of the English language, rather than religion.

The one major exception was the English action in Ireland, where suppression of Catholicism and of the Irish language were concurrent objectives. Queen Elizabeth ordered the suppession of rhymers and genealogists who, she and her advisers held, moved the gentry to rise up against the queen. In the attempt to suppress the Irish language, education was all but eliminated, and teachers took to the hedge schools. The revenge of the Irish on the English for forcing that language on them was to eventually write it and speak it better than the English themselves.

United States culture (religion, art, philosophy and language) is not in immediate danger of being dominated by influence of a mother country, yet in significant areas, continuity and reasoned control are being eroded or placed in jeopardy. The American colonial tradition was for the most part one of religious establishment and of conformity within the respective colonies. Those who did not wish to conform were invited to move on, or in some cases be driven out. Under some duress Roger Williams moved with his dissident religious beliefs to Rhode Island. Others moved west in keeping with the concept of religious freedom proclaimed for the

Massachusetts Bay Colony by Nathaniel Ward, namely that "all Familists, Antinomians, Anabaptists, and other Enthusiasts shall have free liberty to keep away from us, and such as will come to be gone as fast as they can, the sooner the better."

Two main forces gave form to religion as it bore on politics in the decades following the adoption of the constitution. One was rationalism, the theme that had marked the Constitutional Convention, with spokesmen like James Madison and Benjamin Franklin. The other was a continuation of the pietism of the 18th century, marked by individualistic religion, emphasizing personal religious experience as more important than formal creeds and ritual. Despite occasional anti-particular religions over the 200 years of our national existence, religious tolerance generally has prevailed and the line of separation between church and state, if not between religion and politics, has been maintained.

Clear governmental action has been taken against the Mormons for their practice of polygamy, against the Christian Scientists in cases in which obviously medical attention was needed, and against special sects such as snake charmers and drug users. Some claims based on appeal to freedom of religion have been rejected in whole or in part. The courts have allowed state payments for some textbooks in some sectarian schools, and allowed reimbursement of transportation costs for parents sending children to non-public schools, but denied the use of public schools for sectarian services. Prayer in public schools and Bible reading have been declared unconstitutional. Confusion grows with almost every court decision on the church-state issue, but the thrust overall is to limit religious practices, or religious-related practices, once accepted with little or no question. Constitutional amendments have been introduced to allow prayer in public schools and to declare that the United States is a Christian nation, as well as legislation requiring non-Christians who are to hold public offices to take a special oath.

Religion in the United States is fairly secure in its traditional status, whereas other elements of culture are threatened, some by internal, nonrational forces, others as a result of defined and identifiable policy decisions, and others by outside and nonpolitical influences.

John Ahearn of Stanford University, in an address to the graduating class of 1979, identified the condition of the graduating class of that year (and that of the nation) as best covered by the word "entropy." The class, he said, did not know how it "relates to the past or the future," and it "had little sense of the present." It had no life-sustaining beliefs, "secular or religious," and consequently had "no goal" and no "path of effective action." Borrowing a term from the field of thermodynamics, he described the condition as one of "entropy." Entropy, he said, rules the universe. Of the multiple scientific definitions of entropy, one can, acknowledging the limitations of such transfers from physical sciences to the social and political order, apply at least three as having relevance.

One is its definition as a measure of the "randomness, disorder or chaos in a system." A second is its application as a measure of the amount of information in a message that is based on a logarithm of the number of possible equivalent messages. And third, entropy is an indicator of the degradation of the matter and energy in the universe to an ultimate state of inert uniformity. Conditions have not improved since Ahearn's 1979 observations.

The applicability of the first definition to current conditions is clearly demonstrated in politics, especially in military and fiscal policies, such as the choice of Senator Dan Quayle as vice presidential candidate in the 1988 campaign.

The Bush promise of no new taxes as a communication to be received through lip reading rather than vocal transfer, especially in the anticipation of fiscal disorder and budget deficits, qualifies for coverage under the entropic umbrella. The U.S. involvement of men and women, the number approximately 500,000, and arms in the Middle East, whereas, it is not random, has been marked by disorder, contradictions and confusion approaching the chaotic. As the magnitude of the military commitment grew, so too did the magnitude of purpose, from protecting Saudi Arabia to freeing Kuwait, to deposing Saddam Hussein, to destroying Iraq's nuclear arms and germ or chemical warfare capability, real or potential, to protecting jobs and the American way of life.

All were accompanied by varying legal justifications, from being invited by the Saudi Arabians in a variation of the Eisenhower Mid-East doctrine under which the United States could respond to the call of a government (as in the case of Lebanon in the 1950s) if it was in danger of being taken over by a communist force to reliance on supporting United Nations resolutions, a modification of Jefferson's appeal "to decent opinion of mankind" to support the American Revolution to include decent and indecent opinions. Included also are assertions by the president that he has the authority to do what he is doing and has been doing without outside legal support or congressional approval of any formal kind, while we submit to conditions imposed by those whom we are protecting that Christians and Jews involved with their own defense not display crosses or stars that are offensive to Islam. Meanwhile the Secretary of State and other government officials have gone around the world seeking financial support from other countries, notably Germany and Japan, for our military effort and offering financial aid to countries in return for formal endorsement of our military activity, or threatening to withdraw support from countries receiving our aid if they do not support us.

A variation on the declaration attributed to Pinckney during the War of 1812, in his reply to French demand for "Millions for defense but not one penny for tribute," if applied today would read "Trillions for defense, but only billions for tribute."

The Saudi Arabians dictated to the First Lady what clothes she could wear in visiting U.S. troops, and for a short time it even appeared that the president would agree to a decision to remove all U.S. flags from uniforms and other equipment in the Gulf area. And the president makes major announcements about war plans and progress while standing with one hand in his pants pocket and from a golf cart, interrupting his conference with the press by saying, "I've got to go now."

The second and extended definition of entropy is that of messages and of communication which also bear on the confusion of our times. We are the most over-informed, over-stimulated, over-advertised and over-packaged people in history. In one evening of watching television, a viewer can set against each other advertisements urging greater consumption of milk, eggs and beef, against warnings against cholesterol and advertisements for various concoctions promising relief from gas on the stomach, acid indigestion, and other discomforts caused by over-eating or by eating the wrong foods. Major magazines carry editorials on the effect of tobacco as a cause of cancer while running advertisements encouraging the smoking of cigarettes and use of other tobacco products. Or read or hear words encouraging savings as essential to the competitiveness of U.S. industry and finance, bracketed between advertisements urging borrowing and spending on larger more wasteful automobiles. And then turn to the television news, which is by report the major source of information which American people use as the basis for their knowledge of current events, especially from the evening television network programs which are given in triplicate each evening, with additional support from minor networks and from public television.

Then there are late news, early news, news updates, promises of more news to come and news analysis.

Either by accident or carry-over from the movie industry, or because of a measure of honesty, television news is said to be produced. Each major program has a producer, or set of producers. Hidden persuaders are forbidden in television, and there is some limitation on how much time in a news program can be given or sold for advertising. In a half-hour evening program, approximately 22 minutes are alloted for news, with eight minutes allowed for advertising. In one evening program in which Walter Cronkite reported five or six crises, including Three Mile Island, Mt. St. Helens and the hostages in Iran, anxiety, tension, even attention was relieved by interspersed advertisements promising relief from the ravages of age and minor physical discomforts: Tums offered escape from heartburn even while we might be in the process of being radiated; various aids made false teeth more "palatable," held them in place, made them "five times whiter"; Porcelana took, according to the advertisers, brown spots off hands and face; another product enabled a man who appeared to be about 45 years old catch a woman of about 20 in a short race in the sand in 25 seconds, the amount of time allowed for the advertisement; and finally, just before the end of Walter's final "That's the way it is," there was an ad for Ex-Lax. When Dan Rather took over for Walter, there was a subtle change in advertising. Emphasis shifted from consolation and relief from the disabilities of aging. More positive relief measures were promised, such as Nytol and Sominex, along with Preparation H instead of Ex-Lax.

The third definition of entropy, applicable to American culture, generally is that of "degradation into the ultimate state of inert uniformity." It was this form of entropy that Henry Adams had in mind when he wrote that civilization is always threatened by entropy. The number of "possible equivalent messages" increases. Along with the intensification and multiplication of messages at the level of advertising and news, there is intensification and degradation at a higher level of thought and of communication. Digest proliferation and speed-reading, a kind of do-it-yourself digesting, grows in popularity, being taken up by presidents. Eisenhower reportedly worked from digests. The Kennedy Administration was attracted to speed-reading. President Carter sometime after he was elected announced that he had taken up speed-reading, and reported that his retention rate had improved by 50 percent. He did not say what his rate of retention had been before the 50 percent improvement, nor did he report what 50 percent he was retaining. Crash courses in the Great Books continue to be popular, especially with junior business executives. And instant judgments are becoming the rule. Immediately after presidential addresses, or other important speeches or announcements, television correspondents of no particular reputation either from experience or learning rush to their microphones and to their cameras scattered among boxwood or azaleas or holly bushes (if the event is at the White House) to tell the public what has been said, and then analyze it. Meanwhile, Sperry Rand is running advertisements offering to help everyone become a better listener.

We have moved beyond the McLuhan judgment that "the medium is the message." The message is gone. There is little left but the medium. Pollsters rush about to find out what people think about problems, some of which have not yet arisen, or if they have, have not been identified as problems by the persons being interviewed. Measurements of presidential popularity rise and fall like barometric readings in a hurricane season.

More clearly identifiable and definable forces—both internal to the United States and external—bear upon the erosion and confusion of national cultures. One such force is covered by the comprehensive term "multiculturalism." One of the greatest achievements of this nation has been a molding into a common nationality of a multiethnic society drawn from all races and all religions and most of the countries of the world.

The world has looked to us with admiration for our almost unique achievement and we have been proud of that achievement because so much of the rest of the world has either never escaped from separatism or seems determined to revert to it. Traditional conflicts resurfaced in Africa as independence replaced colonial status across much of the continent in the 1960s. The Indian subcontinent has periodically been torn apart by communal violence, which initially led to the partition into the free nations of India and Pakistan and later to the creation of Bangladesh. Even on the small island of Sri Lanka (Ceylon), Tamils and Singhalese are massacring each other; in Cyprus, the Greek and Turkish communities seem again determined to make each other miserable. Even Western Europe, the heartland of "Western Civilization" cannot escape. Basque separatists agitate and set off bombs in both France and Spain; Corsicans blast the French. Even in Britain, Scottish nationalism seeks its own parliament and its own representation in the European Community and the Welsh want recognition as well. The Irish, who spent generations as a tribal people fighting each other, drew together against the English and the relics of the "Plantation of Ulster" in the 17th century, and division in the Emerald Isle still pits Protestants against Catholics. As South Africa moves to abolish the structure of apartheid, the black population is increasingly caught up in violence between the Zulus, the predominant black people, and the powerful Xhosa-dominated supporters of the African National Congress.

Perhaps most ironic of all is the disintegration that has accompanied the collapse of communism in Eastern Europe. The massive economic problems of the Soviet Union are relegated to a back burner. While the leadership in Moscow is preoccupied with holding the USSR together, Estonians, Letts, Lithuanians, Moldavians, Adjerbaizianis and Armenians struggle against the center and against each other. Czechoslovakia and Yugoslavia, nations patched together from the relics of the Austro-Hungarian Empire after World War I, may not survive. Yugoslavia has already descended into a civil war that threatens to revive the horrors visited on each other by Serbs and Croats during World War II and for hundreds of years before.

In the Middle East, the excesses of Shiites and Sunnis fill our television screens. Lebanon, once a small but prosperous sophisticated state with a well-educated, industrious population has completely disintegrated under the pressures of more than 100 private armies, each vowing to defend some obscure variant of religious practice, and "Lebanization" is a word that has entered the language to mean a more extreme version of the old term "Balkanization."

Now the United States encourages separatism from which we, almost alone of the world's people, have been spared. The trend toward separatism has been led by our major social institutions. Education, the law, the foundations, all contribute to the move toward a separatist society. The Rockefeller, Ford and other major foundations pour money today into projects favoring the approved minorities, rather than into those that spring from the traditional European sources.

The campuses are divided apart by the movement to abolish the traditional canon of liberal education based on Western civilization on grounds that it has been dominated by white males, and replace it with a politically correct course of study. Freshman composition courses at some universities are devoted not to the teaching of writing but the raising of consciousness. The movement is spreading rapidly down through the educational structure to the secondary and elementary schools.

One of the most controversial manifestations of the trend has been the proposed revision of the school curriculum in New York state to eliminate so-called "Eurocentric bias." Historians, including Arthur Schlessinger, Jr., C. Van Woodward and U.S. Assistant Secretary of Education Dr. Diane Ravitch have condemned the trend as "ethnic cheerleading on the demand of pressure groups." For speaking out, Dr. Ravitch has been called "a Texas Jew" and "a sophisticated, debonair racist" by one of the most vociferous proponents of Afrocentricism, Dr. Leonard Jeffries, Jr., chairman of the African-American Studies department at City College, New York. In citing the need for an Afrocentric curriculum, Dr. Jeffries spoke of "a conspiracy, planned and plotted . . . out of Hollywood" by Russian Jews "and their financial partners, the Mafia" who "put together a financial system of destruction of black people." (*New York Times*, 8/7/91)

Experts question the efficacy of an Afrocentric education in raising the self-esteem and the achievement scores of black students. Rather they suggest that it may go the way of previous solutions to the gap in the test scores of black and white children, giving parents more power in school governance—which has led to the fragmentation of school districts and vastly increased expense as additional layers of administration must be paid for; teaching the teachers to speak and understand black English didn't work either. Dr. James Comer of Yale University, who has pioneered programs for disadvantaged children in inner-city schools, puts rewriting the curriculum "well down the list" of things that help improve children's self-esteem.

In an article in *Network News and Views* (February 1991), Erich Martel, a history teacher in the Washington, D.C., school system, noted that there is no evidence that an Afrocentric curriculum will improve students' self-esteem. He claims that in the best-known Afrocentric curricula history is more myths and half-truths than history. In each generation, historians look anew at the past and at data that may be susceptible of reinterpretation or reevaluation. As a result, they may modify and even discard ideas that were once accepted. But their work becomes part of the body of historical knowledge only when it is widely accepted by other historians. Martel cites as examples the work of W.E.B. DuBois and John Hope Franklin who, following accepted standards of historical research, formulated new interpretations of historical material that revised the accepted view of the Reconstruction period. Historians, black and white, accepted their views because they wrote not black history, but history.

Immigration is also contributing to a Balkanization process that is taking place in this country. The immigration-generated diversity of recent years has led to a reemergence of ethnic group politics. As the receipt of social benefits—everything from jobs to housing and political representation—becomes conditional on one's membership in a particular racial, ethnic, religious or linguistic subgroup, there are growing incentives not to assimilate.

Assimilation—the gradual shedding of large portions of one's native culture in exchange for admission to and acceptance in a new society—is a difficult and traumatic process under the best of circumstances. It has rarely been completely accomplished by immigrants themselves. It has usually been their children and grandchildren who have completed the transformation from what we today call "hyphenated Americans" to simply Americans. And, for as long as immigrants have been coming to this country, there has always been resistance to assimilation. However, in the past, our society has always demanded implicitly, and often explicitly, that immigrants and their children adopt our common culture and language.

Arthur Schlessinger in a recent book calls "The rising tide of ethnicity [in the United States] a symptom of decreasing confidence in the American future. . . . The cult of ethnicity has reversed the movement of American history, producing a nation of minorities— or at least of minority spokesmen—less interested in joining with the majority in common endeavor than in declaring their alienation from an oppressive, white, patriarchal, racist, sexist, classist society."

In other eras, immigrants were inculcated with the belief that George Washington, Thomas Jefferson, James Madison, Abraham Lincoln, et. al., were no less their patriarchs, as they were the patriarchs of those whose ancestors came over on the *Mayflower*.

Today, as we have set the role of our immigration policy to meet the needs of others, we also question whether we have a right to educate them in our values, or whether we have an obligation to help them reinforce their values, cultures and languages. From the campuses of our major universities to the public school systems of our major urban centers, we are in the process of redesigning curricula to teach immigrants and their children about their cultures in their languages. "The melting pot yields to the Tower of Babel," laments Schlessinger.

If one thinks of the classic definition of colonialism—the arrival of large numbers of people who impose their cultural values and language on the preexisting society—it is hard not to define the current wave of immigration as a colonizing force on the United States. What distinguishes the United States from other colonized societies is that we have the power to prevent it, and choose not to use it. The backward societies of Asia and Africa were powerless to oppose the colonial hegemony exercised by the European powers in centuries past. We, on the other hand, have come to question whether the culture that built a society that has the world beating a path to our doors is even worth trying to preserve.

In this social climate, immigration becomes an instrument of divisiveness, as it imposes new cultures and languages on American society. Those who advocate assimilating immigrants into the culture that made this an attractive country in the first place are often "considered reactionary American chauvinists or risk the worse accusations of racism, cultural imperialism or cultural 'genocide.'"

Multiculturalism as a force today is encouraged and sustains large-scale immigration. In 1965 when Congress reformed our immigration laws to allow people of non-European extraction the opportunity to come to this country, we believed we were offering highly qualified and motivated people of all walks of life the opportunity to become Americans, not merely to live in the United States. Senator Edward Kennedy, who managed the 1965 bill on the floor of the United States Senate, stated at the time: "The cities of America no longer have the foreign neighborhoods, the cultural islands, separate, unassimilated (which are) a drag on this nation."

The sheer numbers that have been arriving since that time, and the cultural climate that has developed, have created precisely the conditions Kennedy had thought were gone forever. As the United States is increasingly settled by immigrants who do not share our culture, and as we are increasingly reluctant to demand that they do, we are in danger of inheriting the unhappy legacy of most multicultural societies. Columnist Charles Krauthammer has written that "America, alone among the multi-ethnic countries of the world, has managed to assimilate its citizenry into a common nationality. We are now losing sight of this great achievement. . . . Our great national achievement—fashioning a common citizenship and identity for a multi-ethnic, multilingual, multiracial people—is now threatened by a process of relentless, deliberate Balkanization. The great engines of social life—the law, the schools, the arts—are systematically encouraging the division of America into racial, ethnic and gender separateness."

Ironically, as the Swedish sociologist Gunnar Myrdal observed in the early stages of ethnic reemergence in the United States in the early 1970s, it is not the immigrants themselves who wish to promote these differences, but rather their spokespersons. Some of these ethnic leaders are people whose families have been in this country for generations. Large blocks of unassimilated immigrants, who look to these ethnic leaders as intermediaries to guide them through an unfamiliar political landscape, are a tailor-made political base. Accentuating racial and ethnic differences is their political bread and butter, and continued large-scale immigration is their path to power. One can sense the impatience in the words of Henry Cisneros, former Mayor of San Antonio: "These population dynamics will result in the 'browning' of America, the Hispanization of America. It is already happening and it is inescapable."

Cisneros' words are the words of classic colonialism. He asserts that: 1) People from outside the United States, in this case Latin American immigrants, have a right to come here. 2) That upon settling here, they have a right to have their values, culture and language made at least co-equal with that of the preexisting population. Moreover, there is the implicit accusation that for the Anglo population to resist either further immigration or the "Hispanization" of the United States would be racist.

Our refusal to recognize or our reluctance to assert the relative merits of our culture and way of life, compared with the immigrant cultures, is surprising. For all its faults, our (Eurocentric) culture is the most open, most democratic, most egalitarian, most inclusive society in the history of mankind.

Encouraging and sustaining multiculturalism, and contributing to the entropic conditions of our society is a more formal, organized, and identifiable force, that of bilingualism or multilingualism.

Our social and political institutions are based, and expected to operate, on a common language or heritage. Our schools have traditionally assumed that English was to be the common language of the United States citizens, regardless of what country or culture they or their forefathers had come from. Public and non-public schools for generations have taken in immigrant children, and the children of immigrants sent them to their English lessons and told them of the Pilgrim fathers and taught them to pledge allegiance to the flag, writes William Pfaff. It was in and through the English language that those new to America learned of our culture and acquired a sense of belonging.

The history of the growth of bilingualism and of multilingualism in the United States is an interesting study of the strange working of ideas, bureaucracy and of politics. Dr. Diane Ravitch, assistant secretary of education, describes the process of politicization. "There is," she writes, "another kind of politic, however, in which the educational institutions become entangled in crusades marked by passionate advocacy, intolerance of criticism, and unyielding dogmatism, and in which the education of children is a secondary rather than a primary consideration. Such crusades go beyond politics as usual; they represent the politicization of educations."

Certainly this kind of politicization has marked the cause of bilingualism to the point that, as a result of legislative action, bureaucratic administration and court decisions, it has become a civil right rather than what it was intended to be when introduced, namely, a pedagogical aid or technique for teaching English, and an act of "affirmative ethnicity," as it has been labeled by Noel Epstein, former education editor of *The Washington Post.*

Bilingual or multilingual instruction is not a new or recent idea in American education. Languages other than English were a part of education early in our national history. The Germans were the earliest non-English-speaking body of immigrants. By 1800 approximately 10 percent of the population of the United States was of German descent. As late as 1900, approximately eight million Germans immigrated into the United States compared to 2.5 million English-speaking immigrants. Instruction in language in German community schools emphasized, both early and late, German over English.

Public school instruction in German existed in Pennsylvania in the 1830s. In fact, in Philadelphia German-speaking Americans were operating schools in German as early as 1694. Sometimes these schools also taught in English, but sometimes they did not. German language instruction promoted social cohesion in the German community. As the educational researcher Steven Schlossman pointed out, "The nineteenth-century German community in America was rent by deeply divisive religious and regional antipathies, yet the issue of native-tongue instruction drew them together more effectively for political purposes than any other."

Most of the early German immigrants were farmers and they settled in Midwestern farms and cities in highly concentrated German-speaking communities. It was only in these rural, densely populated areas of German inhabitants and in a few cities that extensive German language instruction programs operated. Most often, however, only token native-language instruction was offered in these schools.

Wisconsin, which had the highest rate of German settlement, had widespread use of German in the rural schools. The reasons given in Wisconsin, as well as in Cincinnati and Indianapolis, for the use of vernacular instruction in the public schools were similar to reasons used today by advocates of bilingual education: it was thought that children first needed to learn how to express their thoughts in their mother tongue; children should learn to read German first and then learning English would be faster; bilingual skills in English and German would be a boon for foreign commerce; and dual-language education was a nexus to general intellectual development and school achievement.

Another especially convincing argument for the use of German language in public schools came from William Torrey Harris, an early St. Louis superintendent of public schools. Harris was a firm believer in the role public schools played in fashioning Americans out of different immigrant groups. To Harris, the public schools afforded a unifying force in teaching everyone a common language, English. As Harris believed,

> With differences of language there go, also, differences of manners and customs—of feelings, convictions and ideas; the worst of results may be anticipated in a community where difference in language prevents one portion of the community from holding free intercourse with the other. The full protection of one class of the population from another cannot be secured, unless all speak the same language.

Thus, Harris was convinced that by using some German in the public schools, the Germans would not set up separate schools and would avail themselves of a public school education. Harris also argued that "every settler enjoyed an inalienable right to send his child to private schools that entirely excluded English language instruction; however, no one possessed a legal right to ask public schools to teach any language other than English."

Much like the issue of dual language instruction today, there were concerns with how to teach, whom to teach, when to teach, and where to teach the German language in the public schools:

Many critics claimed that German-language instruction had nothing to do with pedagogical considerations, which advocates invoked merely to rationalize political power plays, or with the alleged goal of more effectively assimilating German-American children. Rather the true object was to transform America into a Teutonic paradise where none but purely German customs and modes of thought will prevail or be allowed.

When the United States entered World War I in April 1917, a reaction arose against all things German. The bilingual instruction that emerged in the 19th century did not survive World War I.

After its annexation in 1848, the Territory of New Mexico authorized Spanish-English bilingual education. Pennsylvania, Colorado, Illinois, Iowa, Kentucky, Minnesota, Missouri, Nebraska, and Oregon also passed laws allowing instruction in languages other than English. In the early part of the 19th century, there were also bilingual education programs in parochial schools formed by Italians and Poles attempting to preserve their language and cultural traditions. Moreover, other ethnic groups, such as the Chinese, Japanese, Greeks, and Jews traditionally operated afternoon and weekend schools to teach their native language and culture. After the Civil War, in Louisiana French was also used in the schools in French-speaking areas; Hawaii allowed the use of other languages in schools by petition, and Minnesota allowed instruction in other languages, even though textbooks had to be in English.

Bilingual education in the 19th century always meant utilizing the native tongue of non-English-speaking immigrants. Vernacular instruction was a symbol of German political clout. Its capacity to endure depended on the strength of that clout. Such education was always initiated and funded at the local level and was not conceived of as a compensatory or remedial program.

Today ambiguity surrounds the definition and purpose of bilingual education. Bilingual education can be a curriculum that teaches in the child's home language and also features daily English lessons and is transitional in nature, or it can be a curriculum taught in English, adjusted in speed and complexity to take account of the students' language limitations. Bilingual education can also be a curriculum devised to maintain the student's native language and culture.

During the 1960s, bilingual education was resurrected in the United States for the purpose of educating children of Cubans who had fled to Miami after the 1959 Cuban revolution. Although these children were non-English-speaking refugees, they were a relatively privileged minority as they came from predominately middle-class families.

In the early 1960s, the Coral Way Elementary School in Dade County (Miami) offered an experimental bilingual program to both English and Spanish speakers. The project was endowed by the Ford Foundation. Parents were given the option of enrolling their children in this new program, and most did. The program was in no way compensatory. The purpose was to make both groups fully bilingual. It was after 1965, when poorer Cubans immigrated to Miami, that bilingual education became a compensatory program. The Coral Way project was terminated in 1966, despite its success. It was intended to be experimental, and further funding was unavailable.

Also, in the 1960s, several Southwestern and Eastern school districts (Delaware, Texas, New Mexico, Arizona, California) began experimenting with bilingual programs. Most programs served hispanics only.

Federal support for bilingual education grew out of Lyndon Johnson's War on Poverty, when there was a heightened public concern for disadvantaged Americans. The Elementary and Secondary Education Act (ESEA) was enacted in 1965. Title I of the 1965 Act provided financial aid to local schools for the education of children from low-income families. If desired, that aid could be used for bilingual instruction. Where Hispanic poverty existed, English as a second language instruction or bilingual education (both subsidized by Title I) was given. At this time bilingual education programs were looked upon as social programs to help indigent, culturally deprived, English language-deficient children improve academically.

The National Education Association promoted the theory of cultural deprivation as being largely responsible for the poor school performance of minorities. "After the successful lobbying efforts for the ESEA, some NEA leaders devoted their time and energy to Hispanic educational issues," i.e., mainly Mexican-American children in Texas.

Senator Ralph Yarborough of Texas became convinced of the efficacy of bilingual education when he attended a convention of the National Education Association. Yarborough introduced to Congress special legislation to make funds available for bilingual education. Yarborough and the cosponsors of his bill (senators and representatives from southwestern and eastern states) believed that for bilingual education programs to gain momentum, there had to be *separate* and *specific* funding for these programs.

Senator Yarborough's bill, introduced in January 1967, was known as the Bilingual Education Act (BEA), Title VII of the Elementary and Secondary Education Act. Like the ESEA, it was intended for indigent students and it specifically mentioned that Hispanics were to be the recipients of such aid.

The hearing for the BEA were dominated by discussion of Hispanics in general, with particular emphasis on Mexican-Americans. The dropout rate of Hispanic children, it was argued, was appallingly high. The median number of years of schooling completed by Spanish-surnamed adults was half that of Anglos and considerably below that of blacks. In fact, many had no schooling at all. Everyone at the hearings acknowledged "that the purpose of bilingual education was to enable the Hispanic child to learn English."

The Bilingual Education Act of 1968 was the first official federal recognition of the needs of students with limited English speaking ability (LESA). Since 1968, the act has undergone four reauthorizations with amendments, reflecting the changing needs of these students and of society as a whole. The definition of the population served has been broadened from limited-English-speaking to limited-English-proficient (LEP) students.

There have been about 20 major court decisions since 1970 on the need to provide special language instruments to students who cannot speak or understand English. By far the most important court decision is *Lau v. Nichols*.

The Supreme Court substantiated in the Lau decision that school districts are compelled under Title VI of the Civil Rights Act of 1964 to provide special language programs for LESA children. However, a memorandum issued by the Office of Civil Rights (a subagency of the Department of Health, Education and Welfare) on May 25, 1970, rendered great influence on the Court and underlined its decision. The Office of Civil Rights had decided that:

. . . discrimination against children who were "deficient in English language skills" violated Title VI of the Civil Rights Act (which provided that "No person in the United States shall, on the grounds of race, color or national origin, be excluded from participation in, be denied the benefits of, or be subjected to discrimination under any program or activity receiving Federal financial assistance").

The memorandum directed school districts to do something for students who had English-language deficiencies. Steps had to be taken that "would go beyond providing the same books and teachers to all pupils.

In 1970, the Laus and 13 other Chinese families sued the San Francisco Unified School District charging that the district's language policy violated both the students' constitutional rights to equal protection and the Civil Rights Act of 1964. In 1971, the district court ruled against the Laus and in 1973 the U.S. Court of Appeals for the Ninth Circuit upheld the decision. "The Supreme Court in January 1974 unanimously reversed the rulings of the lower courts, holding that the district violated the Civil Rights Act of 1964 by not offering the students any special programs to overcome their academic handicaps." In other words, the Lau decision held that the Civil Rights Act of 1964 required the schools to give some kind of extra help to students who did not speak English. Justice Douglas, in writing the majority opinion of the court, stated that children who did not know adequate English were foreclosed from any meaningful education.

Bilingual education was not mandated by the Lau decision. It gave the school districts flexibility to use alternative methods. In the preface to his opinion, Justice Douglas wrote:

> No specific remedy is urged upon us. Teaching English to the students of Chinese ancestry who do not speak the language is one choice. Giving instructions to this group in Chinese is another. There may be others. Petitioners ask only that the Board of Education be directed to apply its expertise to the problem and rectify the situation (Lau v. Nichols, 414 U.S. 563—1974).

Although bilingual education was not decreed, advocates of bilingual education viewed the Lau decision to be a legal strengthening of bilingual education policy. U.S. Commissioner of Education Terrel Bell announced these so-called Lau Remedies on August 11, 1975. The Lau Remedies were not a law or a federal regulation, but in practice, however, they had the full force of the federal government behind them, as OCR embarked on a campaign of aggressive enforcement. Judicial decisions made bilingual education not simply an option, as the Bilingual Education Act of 1968 had intended, but a constitutional and statutory right.

The Bilingual Education Act was renewed, altered, and expanded in 1974. The Lau decision and pressure from ethnic groups led to the inclusion of a new definition of bilingual education which stressed native language and culture maintenance. Bilingual educators saw the act as a vehicle for preserving non-English languages and cultures. In the mid-1970s, the National Association for Bilingual Education (NABE) was formed to ensure that bilingual education was institutionalized as an entitlement program.

The Bilingual Education Act of 1974 was pivotal in that it was the first and only time since the enactment of federal educational aid that Congress dictated a specific pedagogical method to local school districts. In the Carter Administration, an influential national study was published which cast doubt on the effectiveness of bilingual education as a pedagogical method for teaching language-deficient students. The study, sponsored by the Office of Planning, Budget and Evaluation, a subagency of the Office of Education, evaluated standardized test data. Directed by Malcolm Danoff, a leading educational researcher at the American Institutes for Research, the report was critical of bilingual education programs. The study sampled approximately 286 bilingual education classrooms in 38 Spanish/ English projects in operation for at least four years as of 1975. Released in 1977–78, it was the first large-scale (11,500 Hispanic students) comparative evaluation of bilingual education in the United States. The study concluded that most programs were planned to maintain minority languages rather than to speed the transition to English. In fact, most of the children knew English and were retained in the program to improve their Spanish. Those who were deficient in English did not acquire English proficiency. Moreover, the children were already alienated and remained alienated from school despite bilingual education programs. In sum, there was no clear-cut evidence that bilingual instruction was helping the Title VII students perform significantly better in either English or Spanish language arts.

Despite conflict, contradictions and confusion, appropriations for the program continued to grow. Funding increased from $7.5 million in 1969 to $68 million in 1974. In 1984, funding came to $139.4 million and in 1989 to $152 million.

Bilingual education programs primarily serve Spanish-speaking students. It is estimated that 80 percent of the students served in federally funded programs are from Spanish-speaking backgrounds. About 40 percent of Hispanic students drop out before finishing high school. Hispanics lag behind blacks and far behind whites as a whole in average educational attainment. Additionally, 59 percent of Hispanic dropouts have left school by the tenth grade. Moreover, Hispanic students drop out at a higher rate than do other language minority students from non-Hispanic backgrounds. Although there was a big decline over the last 20 years in the black dropout rate, the Hispanic dropout rate stayed the same. The major difference between the educational programs of blacks and Hispanics is bilingual education.

In 1980, an internal review, the Carter White House staff asked the Department of Education for evidence that bilingual education programs, mandated by the regulations, were pedagogically effective as a method for teaching English to LEP students. No such evidence was forthcoming.

Conclusion

The bilingual education issue "brings to the surface a number of other political issues relating to immigration official language policy, the future of the melting pot, demographic changes, and ethnocentricism. Federal bilingual education policy has evolved from a minor piece of legislation into a major educational and emotional issue. Today, 30 states have statutes expressly permitting native-language instruction. Of these, nine require it under certain circumstances; 21 provide some form of financial aid to bilingual programs; and most set standards for certifying bilingual or ESL teachers. Although laws in seven states (Alabama, Arkansas, Delaware, Nebraska, North Carolina, Oklahoma and West Virginia) still prohibit instruction in languages other than English, these bans are no longer enforced.

Adversaries of language and cultural maintenance programs oppose the program for the following reasons: it is divisive in that it threatens the national unity that is reflected in a common core of values; it encourages separatism and segregates students; it encourages the continuance of an ethnic subgroup by slowing down its ability to learn English, absorb mainstream culture, and blend into society; it impedes the acculturative process that earlier immigrants underwent.

Dr. Diane Ravitch, writing in the fall issue of *New Perspective Quarterly,* makes a balanced case on multiculturalism, distinguishing it from ethnocentricism, and noting that Asian-American, African-American or Chicano studies need not be divisive or instruments of cultural Balkanization, but rather can be a process through which both the "pluribus" of our culture and of our nation, and the "unum" can be well served.

Margaret Mead years ago made the case against bilingualism, defining it as a formula for divisiveness and as conducive of illiteracy in two languages. "Biligualism," she wrote, "and especially bilingualism developed in some compensatory effort to absorb immigrants, increase social mobility, equalize inequalities, as a step toward openness and membership into the work, can be a trap. It becomes, as so many analyses of past and recent experiments in relationships between majority and minority languages have shown, a worse trap if there is no literacy in the mother tongue."

Tourism

The final evidence of colonial status is emphasis on tourism as a source of income to the colonial population and purchase of summer or retirement homes, or of estates, and especially of horse farms by citizens of the mother country or countries.

The Germans, especially, seem to have stopped off in Ireland to the chagrin of the Irish, who see a disposition to turn Ireland into a kind of retirement and recreational facilities for wealthy Europeans, with the Irish serving as maids and housekeepers, and nurses, as horse trainers, grooms and jockeys, and as dog handlers and gamekeepers, as caddies and groundkeepers, as butlers and waiters, and chauffeurs and doormen, and as entertainers and musicians. And, as a source of exportable surplus professional personnel, especially of nurses and doctors, to meet special needs in the colonial home countries.

President Bush has become a kind of salesman; traveling to Japan to sell cars (a certain lost cause—somewhat like going from Minnesota to Wisconsin to sell butter. He has appeared on advertisements urging the British to visit the United States as tourists, and the administration is offering citizenship in return for investment in the United States.

The United States has not yet begun sending dancing girls and musicians to meet incoming flights from Europeans countries on the East Coast or from Japan on the West Coast. But travel agencies, in appealing to potential visitors, emphasize the cheapness of the dollar relative to German marks and Japanese yen. Prices in stores and in advertisements are, especially on the West Coast, shown in yen. The Japanese are buying retirement home properties and recreational facilities, such as golf courses. The rich Arab oil sheiks are buying estates and apartments and horse breeding farms in the United States, as has the queen of England.

Afterword

Rome

A SECOND WAY OF LOOKING AT THE CONDITION OF THE UNITED STATES, that is not as a colony to the world, is to compare it to the Roman Republic in its years of decline.

Polybius, the Greek historian of the second century B.C., observed that a state can perish from two factors, internal and external. Charles de Gaulle noted the threat to France from the second, when on withdrawing from Algeria, he said that foreign involvements like those in Vietnam and in Algeria were threats to the integrity of France.

With the threat of war with the Soviet Union gone, and our preoccupation with communism as a threat to democratic ideas and governments ended, the danger that we are likely to perish or even decline because of external forces or distractions is minimal. The threat to our institutions, our stability, and our position of leadership and example to the world is internal. History never actually repeats itself, but there are lessons to be learned from the past. It may be later than we think, but it is not too late for us to look to the warning signs.

Sallust, a Roman historian of the first century B.C., reported on Roman society in the process of change. He noted that the earlier, defined divisions of Roman society into patricians and plebians (the common people) and a middle class of small, independent landholders, had changed into something more complex. The middle class had increased in numbers and in influence and had become more complex, made up of businessmen, financiers, manufacturers, builders, tax gatherers (the civil servants of our time). The army had become a permanent, mercenary professional body, made up of people of little or no wealth, rather than a volunteer army, representing in its composition, the classes of society. There were great numbers of unemployed. There were many poor, living on free grain distributions. The rural areas were being depopulated as people from the rural areas of Italy and from the provinces moved to Rome and to other Italian cities. Bread and circuses were offered to quiet and sustain the poor. Farmers and businessmen were in great debt. Serious work was performed principally by slave labor. The burden of veterans' benefits was oppressive. The cost of wars and of maintaining an excessively large military establishment was a great burden. Taxes generally were oppressive. The wealthy were indifferent to the conditions of the country. Politicians and demagogues proposed equality of all as the goal of political action.

Tacitus, writing a century later in the first century A.D., described a society marked by unrest, violence, intrigue, corruption, decline of morals, cultural confusion and disregard for the law. The Roman senate was distinguished by wrangling. Assassinations were frequent. Greed was the market of business and commerce, usury the rule of finance, and as Fletcher Pratt observed in his book *Hail Caesar*, written in 1936: "The supply of trained leaders began to run out just at the moment when the Republic by virtue of its imperial position was most in need of administrators with minds large enough to embrace the problems of millions and long enough to envisage the problem of decades."

How does the United States of today compare with the Rome of Sallust and of Tacitus and of Polybius?

First to be noted is that there is no middle class in the United States, although columnists and political analysts continue to use the term. Rather, we have a small group of very rich, some five percent, and another of the very poor, some ten percent. The great number of Americans is a classless group made up of a varied assortment of skilled laborers, white collar and managerial personnel, professionals and para-professionals, farmers, small businessmen, government employees, etc.

There has been a massive movement of workers from rural areas and from other countries into the cities of the United States. Approximately seven percent, nearly eight million potential workers in the United States, are unemployed. According to a recent report, more than 20 million persons, one out of every 10 Americans, are receiving food stamps, the bread of Rome, with television-watching the substitute for circuses, and special celebrations of military victories as added entertainment or distraction.

While unemployment and under-employment mount, more and more work is performed by a modern equivalent of slave labor—robots and automated equipment, migrant workers, legal and illegal, and by new immigrants and by low paid workers, child labor, and even prison labor in other countries.

Veteran pensions and other pensions absorb a significant amount of national income. A military establishment working with financial and industrial powers of the country operates on a budget of approximately $300 billion a year. Presidential wars are initiated with almost automatic approval by Congress—Vietnam, Grenada, Panama and the Persian Gulf (at least the part of that war that went beyond protecting Saudi Arabian oil supplies, the original and defensible justification for our involvement).

Wars and military actions are now carried out by a volunteer army, which is in effect a mercenary army, with citizens generally exempted from military service. Powerful institutions, principally major corporations, national, international and multinational, operate beyond social or governmental control. Major governmental agencies, notably the Internal Revenue Service, the Federal Communications Commission and the Federal Election Commission, disregard basic constitutional liberties, rights and guarantees.

There is public indifference to politics, as indicated by the fact that in presidential elections nearly one-half of the eligible voters do not participate. There is great disparity of wealth, with the upper ten percent of the population controlling and holding an estimated 70 percent of the personally held wealth, while the remaining 90 percent hold 30 percent. The burden of debt, both private and public, is overwhelming, with federal government debt approaching four trillion dollars, which, assuming 100 million potential taxpayers, would put a debt burden for federal alone, of $40,000 dollars per taxpayer.

Inflation is running near seven percent annually, while interest paid on basic government debt is below five percent, thus offering as an incentive the saving of a two-point annual loss of savings to inflation rather than a seven percent loss. Corruption in the business and financial institutions is widespread, and usury is common.

Our culture is agitated by demands for multiculturalism and bilingualism and multilingualism, and language is under attack from the deconstructionists. The media more and more emphasize the immediate and the sensational, and on critical issues are subservient to popular trends and to government policy, with television operating somewhere between greed and fear of government regulation or loss of license. The Congress is in disarray, with the president disdaining or disregarding constitutional and traditional relationships, and who now is in the market selling arms, possibly military services, selling citizenships and a new offering of pollution rights.

Albert Schweitzer and others have warned that if a people fail to foresee and forestall trouble, whether in the natural order or in the political and social order, they are headed for trouble. The warning signs are numerous and clear. It is not too late to forestall threatening troubles.

Index